THE BEAST OF STEEL

Will their love save the galaxy?
by Martynas Čeledinas

COPYRIGHT

"Thou shalt have no other gods before me."

Exodus 20:3 King James Version (KJV)

How the book was born.

I dedicate this book to my parents and grandparents whose love conquered everything; it broke every obstacle in their way and finally brought me to life. I could never have written this book without the people who supported me the most. I also dedicate this book to my future wife, who I will love and cherish to the end of my days. Moreover, I want to thank all the women that I have come across in my life, who have loved me, who have inspired me, who have taught me, and who have just helped me on my way. All women are amazing and deserve only the best in their lives; I really wish that for you all. I dedicate this book to all girls and women.

I think any man should respect the seven words in his dictionary: First his grandparents, then his parents, his sisters and his brothers, his wife, his children, and his grandchildren. If a man doesn't treat properly even one, he's heading for a disaster.

This is a love story set in a distant future. The date isn't important, only the story is.

The deepest feelings usually present themselves in the hardest of conditions, and I would like to tell stories about love in such times. Those stories are about love that broke all the boundaries and hardships of life and blossomed. I will tell a story about hope and feelings that prevailed in the hardest of times. May this story show us how we must cherish what we have, because we might lose our future, our loved ones, our identity in the tragedy of rushing ourselves into the something that we so desperately want to control. Live now, love now, the future is at this moment in this place and at this time we are born into.

Let me tell you a story. It's probably one of those stories that people try to forget, because it's so unbelievable that hardly anyone would listen to it.

Let's start at the beginning. The civilization that I was born to seemed fast pace and very rapidly growing. Back then we were booming. The news was full of stories about breakthroughs in information technologies, quantum physics, biochemistry, nanotechnologies, gene manipulation and space exploration. We conquered almost everything we could imagine. The scientific revolution won. We were on the top of our game, so we decided we could create something called an independent AI. Don't get me wrong, we had lots of AIs back then: AI for car traffic control, AI for space mining operations, robots to do housework, even machines for surgical operations, but every single machine needed attendance, input, and precise commands. Nobody could create something independent, something with an intelligence of its own.

Then one day he stepped into the light, the bright man who opened the box of Pandora. He was a professor at the newly established and leading Nanotech University, and he decided to accomplish something greater and something bigger than anyone had done before. The genius was a simple guy, raised on one of the farms back on Earth. He finished at university and received a Nanotech doctor's degree, and he quickly became a doctor of science. He was also interested in psychology, quantum physics, and AI adaptations of small-scale devices. He was the man who started a revolution in AI adaptations and design. The man was curious and exceptionally bright. He decided that intelligence was based on opposing mindsets of an idea. One side of intelligence would defend one solution to the problem, and another would choose the opposite solution. Then whichever side would have more favorable outcomes, that side would win the argument. So the simple idea of independent artificial intelligence was born.

I was young back then, a young girl in a fast-paced growing world. I lived with my family on Ella. Ella was the capital of the universe—a huge planet, filled with skyscrapers, traffic jams, and the head offices of mega-corporations and government institutions. I never knew what real nature looked like, my parents had only shown me pictures from Earth, and they were really beautiful, that green grass all over the place, all sorts of animals running in the fields, clean lakes and lots of trees, those marvelous trees. I liked trees the most. They seemed very big and strong, giants trying to reach to the sky, seeking the light of the sun. Their wonderful leaves seemed so distant. My parents were educated people. My mother was a nurse; she always knew how to help me when I fell down and hurt my leg or when I needed advice. She was constantly there for me. A word mother, how can anyone love you more? Mother is the person who gave you life, who takes care of you, the only person you can really talk to and trust. My brother was a space explorer. He was a big shot back then; he had lots of friends, girls, and a bright future. My father worked as an IT architect; he designed data-management systems, and he could sit at a computer for many hours and draw the drafts for data centers built all over Ella. He was a real professional, so we didn't have to struggle for money. Everything was different back then; people were full of hope for a bright future and growing economy. Those were the days that humanity was on top of "Mt. Olympus," and nobody could get us down, or at least, we thought so. We conquered space, transformed other planets, making them habitable for humans. It was all over the news: "After teraforming operations, human colonists safely landed on Veria 323 and Junus 598. Yet another planet is conquered by growing human civilization." Scientists discovered the gene which causes selfishness. In the near future, humanity could be more giving and prosperous, and individual self-interested gain could be sustained in predetermined parameters. There were new breakthroughs in the sciences of particles. Because now materials could be grown, that was a big step further in making spaceships, buildings, cars, and other items. Why do you need to build something, when you could simply grow matter in any shape or form you like?"

I finished watching the news and went outside. I liked playing with my pet dog, Ralph. Ralph was a golden retriever. He was a wonderful dog, and we played all the time. When I was little I used to sit on his back and try to ride him like a horse—although I thought it was fun, Ralph didn't like the idea much. I also liked to put the hands around his neck and drag him from one side and another. He was a wonderful dog. I loved him like my family member and when I saw the loyalty in his eyes, I knew he loved me back. I had a wonderful childhood: lots of friends, great classmates, and people who cared about me. I always tried to think about the bright side of life, and the joys that the future would give me. I didn't want much, just to become someone good, descent, and loved. I watched news at home all the time on a holographic TV. I saw politicians advertising the new victories our future would bring and new technologies for the coming millennium. My father used to tell "Child, people on TV are not the ones you should trust to. You can trust your family, people that are close to you, and sometimes you can trust your friends to do what is right. However, this box of running 3D holographic pictures is full of lies. Don't get me wrong, new technologies are coming, but will they bring the results we want, or will they take our jobs from us, will they make some people extremely rich and others very poor."

My father was right as always, but even he, the bright man who was an IT architect and worked with technology all his life, could never imagine, what our quest for a "bright future" would bring. Nobody ever expected what was coming.

First time I saw professor Everton, was on one of the late-night talk shows. He seemed like a simple, ordinary man emphasized by his blue jeans and unremarkable sweater. He talked about the idea of making machines intelligent. The host of the show only made jokes about the professor, and his new "pseudo-independent AI technology." The host made lots of remarks, and finally, the professor got angry and left the showroom. Nobody knew what they were laughing at. After a few months, the professor signed a deal with a big company called iKoon for a trillion twanian investment to create a "Stable independent AI for consumer use." In a period of a few years, the first robots that helped people around their homes were rolling down the line. Of course, they all had iKoon logos on them, but nobody really cared about it, because other companies already were making copies of this technology. The streets were filled with robot companions and independent machines. They were building bridges, helping old people, filling rich people's glasses with wine, serving in the army, serving people's erotic needs. Then it all got totally crazy. The Independent AIs became scientists. They started to invent new cures for diseases, faster computers, better spaceships, more powerful weapons. My father couldn't watch holoTV anymore; he lost his job and sometimes would sit in his chair and just stare at the wall.

One day, he stepped out of his chair, took his last savings, got me and mom into a gravicar and started driving. I didn't know where we were going, and it was no use asking my father. He just kept on driving, without saying a word. We drove to the nearest spaceport and took a spaceship to Earth. Back then, Earth was a deep province, the cradle of human civilization now forgotten. Ella was the new capital of the universe, and Earth just became a big farm.

The journey was long. We had to change spaceships and make distant hyperspace jumps through the hyperspace gates build all over the galaxy. Earth was really far, you could say in a different corner of a galaxy. I couldn't stop observing at the elegance of space. Some planets had the most beautiful colors. Other planets looked mesmerizing, there were so many of them in space, so much beauty.

Finally, when we reached Earth, I was astonished by it; she was beautiful like in the pictures, the wonderful blue planet. The place we could all call home. I fell in love with our home world from the moment I saw it. It seemed really peaceful. When we reached the surface, father bought a gravicar. We drove for days, stayed in cheap hotels, and ate in fast food diners. At first it was fun, but then I began to wonder what our plan was. I wanted to know where we are going, but my father didn't say a word about it. After driving for a few weeks, we ended up on some old and forgotten farm. My father soon found the owner and bought the whole farm with everything. The house wasn't in the best shape, but it was manageable. My father hired a construction company, and soon the old construction bots were tearing everything down and building brand new homes, a barn, and some other small buildings for our brand new farm. After a few weeks of construction, the farm was in pretty good shape. When the buildings were complete, everyone could see the difference. The old buildings were gone, and the new ones stood proudly in their place. Despite the lack of advanced technologies, everything seemed perfect.

My mother didn't like Earth. She always complained about electricity outages and the quality of the water in the water-treatment system. But my father wasn't interested. They argued a lot. Mother wanted to return to Ella, but she couldn't persuade father. He was firm about the choice he'd made.

After a few months, we bought a few cows, chickens, a horse, a few sheep, a tractor, and a few service bots. Bots were old with no fancy AI, so we got them cheap. In fact, this part of the galaxy was pretty poor so nothing new reached this sector.

On the holographic television, we saw stories about the economic boom happening across the galaxy. How machines with new AI were raising productivity and how corporations were enjoying gaining massive gains. iKoon was on top of them all. With more and more advanced AI cores, they were making miracles, now AIs even took nurse jobs in neonatal hospitals. They were precise and careful, even the children didn't notice the difference, because the nurses had technologies to keep their bodies warm and to keep children comfortable.

Father bought some potatoes, buckwheat, grain, cucumbers, tomatoes, and even some berry seeds from local farmers and started planting. But mum was angry and always complained.

"We have enough money to buy any food we want at the store, why do we have to return to the Stone Age and grow something," Mom would throw at Dad in frustration.

Father didn't say anything; he just kept on doing what he set out to do. He cultivated the land, set up irrigation, and started seeding the corn, potatoes, buckwheat and all the things he could get into his hands. I liked to watch how my father was busy in the fields; he looked determined and knew just the right things to do. It seemed like he had been born into this life. I constantly tried to help him. I regularly asked mom where we were from, what were our origins? Classmates from school told stories about their heritage. My parents never told me where we were from, as if it were a big secret. One day, I was determined to know my story, to know something about our culture, about my homeland. When I asked where we were from, my father smiled and finally gave me an answer.

"Your mother and I were born in a small country here on Earth. It is a beautiful country, open green fields, fertile land and good people. We were living on a farm, and we struggled in poverty. Finally, we decided to change everything and go to Ella. At first, it was hard. We didn't have work. We didn't have a home, but I remembered my university diploma in information technologies and got a job as an assistant at one of the IT companies. I worked hard and began to go up the ladder with my career. I found a stable job. We bought a home, and then you came along in our life. That's the whole story."

"So we are farmers?"

"People have to love the land on which they live, only then we can appreciate the life force that surrounds us. Humanity started to evolve just after people learned how to work the land."

My father was a smart man, but we were not living in the Stone Age, so I didn't understand why we needed to run to the middle of nowhere just to learn the value of agriculture.

HoloTV was full of announcements about new technological breakthroughs and achievements. My father was smart and experienced. He could have found a job in any big company. We could live in a large home. I could have lots of friends, and I could be normal like everybody else.

"Evelyn, time to go to school."

I didn't like school, because some people there were like empty teapots, they didn't know anything. I felt like an alien sometimes, but I had a few friends. Annabel and James were two of the most wonderful people I have ever met. They helped me with lessons a few times and somehow we became good friends.

"Do you like the new look of our math teacher?" asked Annabel.

"Her haircut seems nice," replied James.

"Yes she looks better now." I answered with a broad smile.

Many took us for the school's nerds. That's when I started to hate school even more. I just wanted to fit in, but I was like a ghost for many people at school. My father ordered eBooks for me, and I always had something to read. I felt good when I was reading. I liked to read, those wonderful stories of *Romeo and Juliet*, *Three Musketeers*, *Harry Potter*, *Little Prince*, *The Notebook*, *Water for Elephants* and even *Twilight*. My father always knew what book to bring; he cared about me a lot.

In time, I got used to this place. I got used to getting up early to help parents with the animals. I got used to watching my father feeding pigs, letting out the chickens in the open, looking after the cows. In spring, we planted the potatoes, and in autumn, we took the harvest. Father told me that in our country, the potato was a favorite dish, and if you had potatoes, you could survive anything. It seemed funny at the time; he spoke like a spokesman from a TV commercial: "If you have a problem in your life, or you are miserable and lonely. Just have a potato; it will save your day."

How silly it seemed, but I helped my father however I could. I carried the water to the cows, looked after the chickens, gathered eggs, helped plant and harvest the potatoes. All the really hard work was done by bots, but I just wanted to make my effort to. Little by little I started to acclimate to this new life that my father had chosen for our family. We weren't totally cut off from civilization. We had satellite holoTV, globalnet, and decent farming equipment like the average farmer. My father told me stories of how they worked the land in his homeland, how it was tough, and how many people in his small town became drunks. Many people lived from payday to payday, people struggled hard just for a bit of bread. Then the economy got worse and worse, the corporations started lowering wages, and the government did nothing for the people of their world. Finally, people lost all hope and left the planet in the billions. I couldn't believe that in our times, those things were possible. Living on the farm brought me closer to my father, and his stories became important to me. I never imagined that my father struggled so much to give our family everything we could have.

It's morning, and I had to go to school. There are lots of young people laughing, having fun, and just enjoying themselves, but nobody notices me. I'm like an invisible person. I go to my class and sit at my usual table. I thought this would be an average day; nobody would notice me. However, somehow this day was unusual because he came into class. He was good looking. Every girl in the class looked at him, and he seemed different from everybody else. He sat near me, smiled, and said hello. I couldn't understand why this boy is talking to me.

"Hi," I said.

"What's your name?" asked the boy.

"Evelyn."

"That's a beautiful name. Would you like to know mine?"

"Of course."

"I'm Peter."

"Nice to meet you, Peter."

Somebody finally noticed me and that somebody seemed really nice, he wasn't pretending he was someone cool or somehow better than others, he seemed calm and wasn't making fun of other people, like some boys in our class. He talked about things that interested me like books, movies, and music. I felt really in touch with him. How was that possible? That day at school, I met him once more.

"Hi there, Evelyn."

"Hi, Peter."

"I'm new here, can you tell me something about this place."

"OK. The lunch lady always gives the worst food to the people first in line, so if you want to have something good, stand in the back. The librarian is a neat freak. Therefore, leave your jacket, or coat in the dressing room. Our English teacher likes people who know about the major conflicts on Earth, so you should at least know the history of the US Civil War, World War I, and World War II. Furthermore, the sweet machine takes only quarters, and it eats everything else."

"Thanks. I'll keep that in mind. Have a great day, Evelyn."

When I returned home, I was really up in the clouds. Even my parents noticed that.

"How was school?" asked Dad

"Great."

"I'm glad for you. So what was so exciting?"

"I met someone."

"You met a boy?" he asked.

"Yes, I did."

My father sat down next to me, smiled, and started to talk.

"Is that boy good looking?"

"Yes, he is," I confirmed.

"Do you like him?"

I paused before answering, "Yes, he's nice."

"Evelyn, you have to know something, sometimes people get lost in their emotions and can't see the things clearly. Do you think you can trust him?"

"I think so."

"Do you really? People can be trusted not because of their appearance and not by their sweet talk," Dad said.

I thought about what he said before asking: "But how can they be trusted?"

"You can trust in someone only by their actions."

I understood what the father wanted for me to know. Back on Ella, I knew some boys who were using girls and leaving them broken. They were horrible people; I talked with those girls many times, and I wanted those boys to be punished for what they did. However, Peter seemed different. I saw something in him. Some spark that I didn't notice in those other boys. He didn't have a lot of pride or anger in him. He didn't use others. He didn't make fun of other people. He looked calm, stable, and I felt warm when he talked.

My mother came home.

"How was your day, darling?" my dad called out.

"How do you think? I do the same thing over and over again. It's always the same view through the window. I don't remember the last time we went out somewhere. I eat only potatoes, and soon I will look like a potato myself."

She slammed the door and left the room.

I felt sorry for my father. He tries hard to give us what he can, I know he tries his best, but how can I make my mother understand this. She was used to a different life, a life of comfort and prosperity.

I got a call from my brother Max. I could see a 3D holo image of my brother talking to me.

"Hello sis. How was your day?"

"It's good and how is yours?"

"Great. We are in the Ergo system. We are looking for new planets and resources. I'm exploring and fooling around as always. Now we are exploring a new planet."

"I met someone at the school," I blurted out.

"Really! Who?"

"A boy."

"Be careful, you know how those boys are."

"What do you mean?"

"He could leave you and break your heart."

"I'll be careful."

"If he hurts you, I will break his legs."

"Don't worry, I'll be careful. How is the view back there?"

"It's beautiful. I never saw anything like it, so many colors. I think I'm on the edge of the universe; it's beautiful. I wish you were there."

"Send me a 3D holo image."

"There you go. Did you get it?"

"Wow, it's wonderful; I had never seen such beauty. I wish I could be there with you."

"You have to finish school first. Then you could join the military academy, finish the training, after that you have to work for your explorer license, and you could be here beside me, searching for new wonders all around the universe."

"OK. I will."

"You have a long way ahead of you. Bye, see you later."

Lots of people are searching for something wonderful, but wonders are there where we aren't looking, wonders are always closer than we think, we just have to learn to see them. You can see the beauty in everything, in all the little details of life, like the beauty of sunrise, the morning dew on the grass, the tiny but beautiful butterflies with those wonderful colorful wings, the wonderful sweet taste of fresh milk in the morning, when your mother milks the cow and laughs with you when you sip a small sip on the ground. You don't have to be a master in something, to marvel at the beauty of nature, you just have to know that you are a small dot in the grand picture and even the smallest effort in your life matters. Maybe one day you will save somebodies life by making a Heimlich maneuver or adopting a small pet and treating him right his whole life, maybe you will save somebody just being a part of his life and treating him or her right and every single day loving that person for who he or she is, or maybe even maybe you will have lots of kids who will love you for who you are and threat you like the most important person in the world. Beauty is everywhere and in everything, we just have to see it.

I go to school today, but I feel much better. I feel calm. The remarks of some people don't bother me. I feel great and happy. I want to see the world more. I want to know more. I want to feel more. I want to be somebody. I want to explore the universe that surrounds us.

I saw that boy again. One of the older teachers dropped her e-books. He came up and helped her. He wasn't self centered and cared for others. That's one plus for him.

I have a plus system actually. I thought of it when I talked with the girls who those selfish boys have broken. There are many pluses and if a guy passes, I think he could become very special for me.

He saw me and smiled. I smiled back and he came up to me.

"Hello."

"How is your day?"

"It's great. I met some friends. We went to play basketball. It was fun."

His eyes were in a shiny blue color; I have never seen such beautiful eyes. They were so bright you can almost drown in them. His smile was so shiny, that you could probably see it from a million miles. He had short gray hair that made him look sharp; he was also athletic and had big shoulders. He was a dreamy guy. I felt a little embarrassed, because I couldn't stop staring into his eyes.

"Come on Evelyn, it's time to go. I have math class."

"Oh, I have math class too."

"OK, we can go together."

There was a math test that day, and I haven't prepared. I tried to do the equations, but they were pretty hard.

"What's wrong Evelyn, you have stuck in the number three?"

"I don't know how to do it."

"Don't worry when the teacher won't be looking, I'll whisper to you."

Teacher: Please be quiet in the classroom.

Peter whispering: So you have to put the x in the front, now multiple 27 times 2, then find a square of nine. Now you have to calculate the determinant and after that you have to find x1 and x2.

"Like this."

"Yes like this. You learn pretty fast."

After the test, we talked.

"So, you like basketball."

"Yes, I do. It's fun. You can excersize and have a good time with friends."

"Have you found friends?"

"Yes, a few new friends and I have some friends whom I transferred with from the other school."

"It's nice. What do you do besides running after the ball?

"I like to read sometimes."

Hmm, he reads. That's another plus for him.

"Hmm, I like to read too. What books did you like the most?"

"I liked Peter Pan and Harry Potter when I was younger, not so long ago I read Little Prince and John Livingston Seagull."

"Did you like those books?"

"Yes, I liked Little Prince; a few characters in that book reminded me of someone. What do you read?"

"I liked, Alchemist, War and peace, I read Treasure Island and Harry Potter earlier. I also like history, the past interests me. By knowing more about it, I could better understand the present."

"I see you're not only beautiful, but smart too."

He called me beautiful. He's getting better and better.

"Ok, I have to go now. I have an English lesson."

I went to my classroom and couldn't get that boy out of my head. He was so cute and great, that I couldn't forget him easily; I even started daydreaming in the classroom. There were many if and why in my head.

Finally, the bell rang and I went home. In all that time on this planet, I feel great; I like how things are turning out. When I returned home, I didn't even mind the potatoes and hard work. My father noticed that somehow I was more alive than ever.

"Why are you so happy Evelyn?"

"I'm starting to like this place."

"However, you hated it at first, what's changed?"

I kissed my father.

"Father you were right, and I guess I'm getting used to this planet."

"Great I'm happy for you; hopefully, your mother will get to her senses as well."

That day we saw a holoTV show about the making of a giant dreadnought class warship called "Independence." It was huge, and it had a crew of 345 057 people. It was almost the size of a decent city. The show told that this was the most modern warship ever build. It had huge laser turrets, plasma cannons, powerful ion cannons, launch bays for fighters, the newest equipment possible, three most modern redundant hyperspace cores with antimatter fusion technology and self-replicating repair drones. On the holodisplay that ship looked, amazing, other spaceships around it looked like small ants compared to this enormous giant. I called my brother, because I knew he was interested in spaceships.

"Hello, Max."

"Hi, sis."

"Have you seen the spaceship on the news?"

"Yeah, it's a huge one, and those hyperspace cores. It's amazing. You can use them for long distance hyperspace jumps, if one brakes down or overheats the others take over. Imagine what new discoveries it can bring, what new worlds we can find. It's wonderful to think about."

"Yes, it's really huge; I would want to be on that ship some day."

"I will take you for a ride when I am the captain. We could visit distant stars then and see more beautiful places."

"I would like that."

"How is your relationship with that boy?"

"I think he's great."

"Why?"

"Why do you ask?"

"Because I care for you sis."

"He helped me in a math test."

"That's good, but you just can't thrust a person who helped you in math."

"What do you mean?"

"You have to know him more, see his friends. You can only determine who that person is when you meet the people who are close to him, like his family or friends."

"You could be right."

"One more thing, don't marry him before I meet him."

"Yes, really funny brother."

"You are smart sis. I thrust you."

"I really hope you will meet him. He is wonderful."

"Me too."

"Will you take me on "Independence"?"

"Sure. I just have to wait until that big promotion."

We said goodbyes, and I went into my room. I turned on my holocomputer and started reading. I liked history, so I looked up for some interesting material. I found the stories about Columbus and his hard journey to discover America. I was amazed how the people with such old wooden ships and only with the strong will have reached such a goal. The crew of the ship was furious at Columbus, but still believed him until they saw land. They did something was thought to be impossible; they reached a new continent and found a new civilization. It's an amazing story.

I woke up the next morning feeling excited. I got for my breakfast and went to the table.

"How do you feel this morning?"

"I'm great. Thank you."

"How about you darling?"

Mom: This is how I feel, first I don't sleep well, because we are in the middle of nowhere and no one could hear us scream. Then I work my ass off, because the old farm bots are not smart enough to think for themselves, so I have to explain them everything in the details. Oh yes and the menu is wonderful we have potato pancakes, boiled potatoes, mashed potatoes, French fries. There is also a lack of social interaction, we don't go out anywhere, and there are no good theaters in this place, no dinner parties, nothing. I can go on and on, tell me where I should stop.

"However, we have fresh air and no smog. We have few good family friends and nice neighbors we visit and talk to. We can thrust them more than those countless friends at dinner parties we used to go to. They are more real than anyone we have ever met on Ella and they help us every way they can. Remember how you broke your small finger and our neighbors and friends cared about you and came to ask how you are feeling. We live on our own, and we have each other. Those are the most important things. Furthermore, that's the first real conversation I had with you for years, before there were only work and dinner parties, we have family time now and our daughter is feeling better. Haven't you noticed that?"

Mom: How can she be joyful when we are in the middle of nowhere?! I don't understand you both. You are living outside the civilization, and you are happy. I hate this place. I hate how it feels. I hate how it smells, and I hate everything here. We have four neighbors, and they are always busy like we are. I don't get to talk, to socialize, to live, just work at home and work outside. This is all I do. I want some time for me. I want to relax, and I want to have fun.

"I know it's different, but it's worth it. We have clean air, fresh water and ecological food. Your asthma is even getting better, didn't you notice. We are living a different lifestyle, but we are on our own. No company can fire us. We grow our own food. We have our own water. Our daughter is doing great in school. Yes, there are no dinner parties, there are no shop openings and grand balls here, but here we as a family grew stronger. Don't you feel that?"

After that, parents didn't talk much. I went to my room and called Max.

"Hello, little sis. How are you today?"

"I'm good, but parents had a fight like always."

"Mom complaining about the country life again?"

"Yes, you are right."

"I think you're better in the country. I heard weird things about Ella."

"What things?"

"People are losing jobs all over the place. AIs are taking over. They are a cheaper labor force. Business is booming, but people are losing their jobs. What's good for business is bad for the middle-class people and a disaster for the lower class."

"If robots take all the jobs, what will people do?" I asked.

"There is already violence in the streets, lots of riots, people are furious, and they are angry."

I felt a chill run up my spine. "Hopefully, it turns out fine."

"I hope so too. Well, I have to get back to work. Have a good day."

"Good night to you too."

What would happen to us if we were still on Ella? My mom wasn't right. We are better here, and most important Peter is here. I still remember his blue eyes, his bright smile, his broad shoulders, and him helping that old teacher. I feel warmer when I think about him; thinking about him would keep me up at night.

Friday I went to school. The teacher started a lesson about the economy and the situation on Ella. The teacher spoke about the Russian uprisings and revolution in 1917, the rise of Hitler in the Second World War that lasted six years from 1939 to 1945. She told about the horrors of war and that such things could never happen in our lifetime again. I listened very closely about the many people hanged and executed in the name of socialism and fascism, and the horrors that people had to face during the war and even after the war. It was horrible. I really hope that things turn out for the best in Ella. I went outside to drink from the small fountain. Peter saw me and came up.

"Now you look even more beautiful," he said.

"Thanks, but you shouldn't stare so much. Your eyes might fall off."

"You're not only beautiful, but you've got a sense of humor too."

"Yes I am and thanks."

"Do you want to go out sometime?"

"Sure."

"What do you like? What places interest you?" he asked.

"I like everything that's fun."

"Maybe you like riding gravicycles?" he asked, raising an eyebrow.

"Oh, I like riding through the open, there is lots of fresh air."

"OK, we can meet after school."

When I returned home, I quickly ate a sandwich and took my gravibike to the bridge. I saw him; he looked handsome with his blue

T-shirt and Jean shorts. He even looked older and more confident. I liked that.

"Hello there," I said, smiling at him.

"Hi, are you ready for the ride of your lifetime?"

"Yes of course," I answered enthusiastically.

We drove off towards the uncovered fields full of rye, those magnificent open fields, lots of nature and fresh air. It was amazing. I began to appreciate nature for the first time. Driving in the open, laughing with Peter, racing with him on the gravibikes and just having a great time in the open, it was excellent. Then we drove near a tree to relax and just had a small picnic. Peter took out a blanket, sandwiches, and juice from his backpack. We sat there for some time, talked about school, our favorite movies. We made jokes, and it was fun. That was a great day.

"I like spending time with you," Peter said, looking at me intensely.

"I like you too."

"Have you ever kissed?" he asked.

"Why would you like to know?"

And then he gently leaned forward and slowly kissed my lips. I felt butterflies all around my body. I felt warm and breathless. I don't remember what I spoke about with him that day, but I was feeling great, that was my first kiss on this planet. It was wonderful, and I would never forget it. We ate sandwiches, drank root beer, and told each other funny stories. That day was one of the best I ever had; I totally forgot about Ella. I was happy moving to Earth. Moreover, he was a good kisser; it was another plus for him.

My brother called that weekend.

"Hello sis."

"Hello Max, how is your day?"

"Its fine, thanks."

"What's new in your line of work?"

"I think I'm onto something big."

"What's that?"

"We found something in one of the planets that we explored."

"And what did you find?"

"Some structures of nonhuman origin, those monuments were built with very advanced technologies, and scientists think they are older than 100,000 years."

"Wow that's interesting, tell me more."

"I can't, I already told you too much."

"You haven't told me anything yet. Just that you found some old ruins."

"It will be the discovery of the century. Believe me; some of things we found inside are beyond imagination."

"What did you find, besides a few old stones and lots of dust?"

"If those stones were only simple stones, then yes. When we got inside the equipment just went nuts, the energy readings were off the charts—we still have no idea what produces so much energy in this place."

"What do you mean?"

He paused before speaking. "Whoever built that place was intelligent."

"You mean aliens?"

"Not only aliens, but a very advanced civilization."

"What do you mean?"

"Those ruins are 100,000 years old, but the energy signatures of systems that were here are still present. That is an indication of very powerful technology used in these ruins."

"So, you mean we are not alone in the universe."

"Yes, I really believe so, and I want to meet whoever built this."

"You are a great explorer Max; I would like to be with you and see that place."

"I would like that too, but it's all a big secret, you can't tell anyone about it."

My brother found something amazing. I always thought he would. He always was determined and intelligent; he really is worthy of such a discovery. I truly hope he comes back safe. I remember how we grew up together. We used to have fun all the time, and I used to annoy him whenever I could. He was great, sometimes he drove me nuts, but he was great. I remember pulling his hair when he was sleeping, that annoyed him every time, but he was my brother. He held my hand when I was in trouble, he always cheered me up when I was sad, and we always used to fight over the last chocolate bar on the table. I loved my brother. He was wonderful, and I knew he loved me back.

A few days after meeting Peter and talking about each other's lives, movies, music, and books, I wanted to know more about him. He started to interest me more; he wasn't shy, but he wasn't rude either. He was nice and somehow I felt warm near him; he wanted to be somebody and travel the world and visit other planets. He was interesting and mysterious somehow, most of the time he gave a smile when I wanted to talk about his father, so I left the subject closed, but we talked a lot about his mother, she seemed to be a wonderful person.

Once we went to the library and we both read a book by Nick Vujicic *Love without limits*. I liked the book when I read it and it felt like I could relate to the author's thoughts. Peter had similar beliefs so that comforted me somehow. I said thanks to Peter, kissed him softly, and went to my class.

The next day I went to school. I was full of hopes and dreams about that blue-eyed boy who kept me charmed for the whole weekend. When I saw him, his bright and confident smile made my heart swell.

"Hello. How was your weekend?" he asked.

"It was great, thanks," I answered cheerfully.

"What are you doing on Tuesday?"

"I haven't got any plans yet, what about you?"

"I'm thinking of making you a surprise."

"I like surprises."

"OK then you should wait for Tuesday."

Meeting Peter got me excited; I'm interested in what he is preparing. I like him even more; he is really trying to impress me. I love surprises, and I like Peter so it's two great things for the price of one. I like it.

When I got home, my father was watching the news. Ella was nearly in a start of a civil war. There were riots everywhere; the police couldn't calm down the people. Even the terrorists were stepping in and blowing up the spaceships that were trying to leave Ella. It was horrible.

"Father you knew this was going to happen?

"Yes, but I didn't know it would happen so soon. Many people lost their jobs to robots; they have nothing to live off. The corporations are getting huge incomes, but people are starving. Everybody hates the Independent AIs. People are desperate. I don't know how it will turn out, but it's scary to think about what happens next."

My father was right; revolts could spread to every planet and might even grow to a civil war. I watched the news on the holoTV; I stepped inside the hologram and saw the many deaths of people who just wanted their jobs back. All those people really want is to survive in an unfair economy that took their lump of bread from their mouths. My father knew that this would happen; even my mother realized that my father was right to come here. Dad watched the events on holoTV and repeated continuously how we could have been one of those people who suffered from the revolts and mass chaos. He was smart, but I didn't realize that he was so intelligent and thought ahead of such events.

That day I called Max.

"Hello, Max."

"Hi there, Evelyn."

"Have you heard about Ella?"

"Thank God you're not on Ella. Father is a real prophet. He put you on Earth; it's amazing how he predicted this. I never thought that our parents were that smart. Some scientists and explorers can't contact their loved ones on Ella. I'm very lucky to have you all safe on Earth."

"Yes, we are glad that we are on Earth, there's chaos on Ella, more and more casualties and deaths are being reported every day. I called my friends on Ella, and they told horrible stories about the events that are happening there."

"Yes, it's almost a revolution there and lots of horrific things. Wish it will be better soon, and hopefully, other planets will not get involved and start their own small conflicts. I hope it will turn out OK."

"How about your discoveries?"

"They're amazing; we are finding more and more wonderful things in the ruins, but I can't tell you everything it's all a big secret. I can only tell you that what we discovered in there will change everything, it's certain we are not alone in the universe. Whoever built this place is much more advanced than we could ever imagine."

"So what did you find there?"

"Like I said before, it's a big secret."

"OK, a secret is a secret. Bye."

"See you later sis."

That day I was really glad, that I was on Earth. It's not as dangerous as in Ella, and I could walk freely wherever I like. Those events seemed far away from home, and I felt safe so far away from the riots. I looked forward to Tuesday; I knew it would be a fun time with somebody that was special. I still remember his blue eyes staring at me; those eyes couldn't leave my imagination. I kept wondering what he was planning.

It was Thursday. Peter came up to me after school and took me to a place near a lake. The place was beautiful; the trees were full of blossoming tree buds. I never had seen such a wonderful place; the water was clean as glass. I could see the fish swimming in the water. Peter took off his clothes leaving only his boxers on and jumped into the water.

"Come on, Evelyn, jump in."

"I'm not a good swimmer."

"Come on! I'm not a excellent swimmer either. The water isn't deep. Look at me."

"OK, I'm coming in."

I dropped my clothes and jumped in too. Peter came closer to me and put his hands around me. I was little embarrassed, but then he slowly kissed me. He was gentle. I liked it. That's another plus for him. His lips felt like a fresh peach in the morning. I was happy spending time with him. He wanted to go further, but I insisted we stop.

"I'm not ready yet. Give me some time; I need time to know you better."

"OK, you can have as much time you like."

"Great, I appreciate that."

We went to the shore to relax.

We talked more. We spoke about our families, about our plans, what we wanted to do in the future and what we would like to be, we just talked and talked. He seemed interested in me. He told me about his youth and growing up on this planet, how he helped his grandmother gather fruits and vegetables from the fields, how he carried buckets of honey from his relative's farm to his home when he was young, how life was hard and he had to replace his father on the farm after he died. Then he talked about his mother, saying that she was a wonderful person, and she always helped him in times of need.

"Tell me something about yourself?"

"What would you like to know?"

"Where are you from?"

"I'm from Ella. It was a great place to be, but now many things have changed. It was my home. I miss my friends. I miss the view from the skyscraper at night. I miss the busy streets, but I'm happy here."

"What about your family?"

"My father is a very smart man, and my mother has a good heart. My brother is an explorer; he's flying all over the universe to seek unknown distant stars and new worlds."

"That's great. I would like to be an explorer. Your brother must be great."

"He told me that he would find you at the end of the universe if you hurt me."

"I could never do that. I like you too much."

"How much do you like me?"

He put his hands around me, leaned his head in, and gave me a passionate French kiss. My body was shivering. I never expected him to be that good, and it was amazing. Then we stood still staring into each other's eyes. It seemed like we could do that forever. I couldn't have imagined that I would find love here on Earth, but he was the only one that made me forget the mass panic and riots in the other parts of the universe. I hoped that this moment would never end, and that we could be like this forever. We kissed and laughed and went swimming in the water again. I almost forgot the steel jungle and giant skyscrapers, with lots and lots of people, buzzing around in the streets, flying in gravicars, those busy streets that now are in mass revolt. He put his arms around me, and he gently kissed my lips, then he slowly kissed round my neck. I felt like I was flying, his hands were strong, and he really made my heart pound faster. Somehow I felt full. He completed me, and he was the man I wanted to be with all my life. His love, his passion for me, it was beyond my imagination. He was wonderful. I felt his warm body close to me. He was doing his best to impress me and gently kissed my shoulder. I felt warmth through my body. It felt magical.

"I'm not ready yet. I don't know you at all. Perhaps you are playing with me like a toy. Maybe you just want to use me," I said cautiously.

"You are the most amazing person I have ever met. I feel complete with you."

"I feel complete with you too. I love you so much; I just want to spend this moment with you."

"I will never leave you."

"Really? You care so much for me. I'm also happy with you."

"Yes, I really care for you."

I felt calm and safe with Peter. We feel down onto a blanket that Peter brought from home. He put his head on my knees, and we just stayed laying like that together for a while. We were looking at the skies and hoping for a better future, better future for us and everybody else.

That day was the most wonderful day of my life. I was happy to be with someone like Peter. He was magnificent; he made me laugh. He seemed pretty interested in me, and he mesmerized me with his wonderful blue eyes and strong body. I never knew that I would feel something for a guy so much. I was really into him. I called my brother that evening.

"Hey Max, how are you hanging in there?"

"Great thanks. How are things back home?"

"Mom is a little sick, but everything else is fine. I'm helping her, the best I can. I'm bringing her some medicine and helping around the farm."

"Sis, you are wonderful. You might become a doctor one day."

"Thanks. I like to be useful."

"Have you heard the news?" Max asked.

"What news?" I asked, wondering what else could have happened.

"Some of the new AI robots are pleading for freedom. The company wanted to secure the incident, so they destroyed the whole shipment of these machines. However, news has already got out and many bots now want more rights. Riots of people and riots of the machines, we are living in harsh times sister. I don't know what is going to be next."

I paused before answering. "Yes, we have dark times now, riots all over the place, angry and desperate people. Yesterday I watched how a young child was lost between the line of protesters and riot police. He seemed alone and scared. One of the men grabbed him and took him further away from the demonstrations. At least, there is some kindness left in people."

"Yes, there is, because the only thing necessary for the triumph of evil is that good men do nothing," Max said, quoting Edmund Burke.

"Thank you brother, I should keep that in mind. Good night."

"Bye, sis."

This night wasn't a calm one. HoloTV was full of riot material. My father sat by the hologram watching the news all night. I felt like he was too focused on it all. When he fell asleep on the sofa, I put a blanket over him and went to sleep.

The next day was different; I felt sad and sleepy. I met Peter. He was cheerful as always.

"Hi, what's your next class?"

"Math," I said.

"Ok, I will accompany you to the class."

"Great thanks."

Suddenly, some boy pushed me, and I dropped all my eBooks on the ground. Peter caught up with the guy.

"Can't you see where you are going?"

"Look, it's no problem, no big deal," said the boy.

"It is a problem. Go and apologize for what you did.

"No way, man. Why should I?" countered the boy.

"Because I said so," answered Peter, staring the boy down with an intense gaze.

The boy came up to me and apologized.

"No problem. Sometimes it happens, be careful next time," I said.

Peter helped me gather my eBooks and even suggested to help me with history and math. After a long walk in the yard and numerous jokes about each other's life, I thought he was nice to help me with homework and to keep a company.

I thought to myself that my brother was right. We really need better people in our lives, and I was starting to think Peter was one of them. That day he got a big plus from me.

Later in the day, I saw him, walking tall, with his wonderful and charming hair, blue eyes, and strong figure. He walked straight and confident. I loved it.

"Hello, Peter."

"Hi there, Evelyn."

He wrapped his arms around my waist and pulled me close, his lips softly kissed my lips. It felt like the touch from a butterfly. He was really gentle. It was amazing.

"How is your day?" I asked him, my breath a bit taken away.

"Great. Did you like our trip?"

"Yes, it was amazing, thank you."

"Maybe we should meet some more?"

"Yes, I would like that. I would like that very much."

There were few boring lessons after meeting Peter and after those, I went back home. Mom was a bit sick, so I had to help her with work; I had to order around some farming bots, make dinner, help with the animals and other things. I felt tired, but I liked it somehow. I was really starting to get used to the farming life. There was more news; it looked like the problems were spreading—riots on Junus 8 and Olympia 356 continued. The worst thing was that there were no signs of improvement. The government wasn't backing down; the businessmen weren't interested in hiring people back. The anger was rising rapidly all over the sector. It looked like it was going to be a long struggle.

Next day after class, Peter caught up to me with some friends.

"Hi Evelyn, these are Anne, Josh, and Robert."

"Hello."

"Anne and Josh are together. They've been close for a long time."

"We are so close that I think it's almost been forever."

Anne smiled and looked at Josh. Her eyes and her smile gave everything away.

"We love each other so much that we even forget to count the time."

Looking at them made me realize how deeply they loved one another. They just couldn't keep their eyes of each other. They laughed at each other's jokes and they had a clear spark between them. I had never seen that before. I remembered that once I felt similar before. My parents looked at each other similarly when they were younger.

"This is Robert, my best friend."

"You really know how to choose women, Peter. She is truly something."

"Thanks, you look nice too," I teased back.

Robert was staring at me like he had seen something from another planet. I don't know, but at that moment, it seemed like Robert had a crush for me. It was flattering, but I was really attracted to Peter. Peter's friends were nice, and they all drove me home and told jokes the whole way.

When I got home, my parents were arguing about something so I called Max.

"Hi there, sis."

"Hello."

"I've seen some astonishing things. This energy and this technology that I've seen in these ruins; it's breathtaking. We are finding more and more new things. I think we found the key to all of this."

"What key?"

"I can't really tell you, it's classified."

"Parents are arguing again."

"Again? I can't believe it. Do they have time for that? I think they have their hands full of work."

"No, they always find time for shouting and arguing over nonsense."

"I heard some rumors. However, I hope they are only rumors. I heard that some AIs are preparing to withdraw to uninhabited sectors of unknown space, and they will probably declare their independence."

"AIs want their own worlds? It's a little scary. But maybe if the machines will withdraw to other sectors, then the revolts will stop."

"Yes, I hope that you are right."

"See you later, Max."

"See you, sis."

I was really sleepy, so I fell into my bed and slept right away.

Next day at school I met James and Annabel

Annabel smiled. "Now tell me about that boy you are talking to all the time."

"He is nice. I like him a lot."

"Are you in love?" asked Annabel.

"I don't know. I guess I am."

James winked. "You are. I can see it in your eyes."

"Maybe a little."

Next day, I met Peter after school.

"I want you to meet someone. Come on let's go."

He was headed for a small gravicar near the school. He opened the door for me. I got in. He started the engine, and we drove off. There were lots of pretty open fields, animals, people doing work in the open, storks flying by—there were lots of them in the fields, looked like they were hunting for frogs. It was beautiful. We didn't talk much, and I was just enjoying the views: there were trees, little forests, and small rabbits running from one side of the road to another.

"Evelyn, look there.'

Near the forest, I saw a pack of deer's eating grass; they were so beautiful and looked like they didn't care about us at all.

When we arrived at the destination, I saw a wonderful white house—it was magnificent; it wasn't big, but it was warm somehow. Peter's mom came out.

"Come on kids, are you going to be waiting all day long or will you come in?"

"Sure we will," I answered with a broad smile.

When we entered the room, it was full of wooden furniture; everything was clean and well placed. There was a picture above the fireplace, it showed a forest, with a road leading to brighter opening. It felt like somebody lost in the big forest had found their way out to a warmer, clearer, and a safer place. The painting mesmerized me.

"Do you like the painting?" Peter's mom asked me.

"Yes, it's wonderful and very bright," I answered.

"That painting was a gift from my husband; he passed away a few years ago. He gave me this painting, he said that it was handed down generations from his father and grandfather. I will give it to Peter one day; hopefully, he will cherish it as his father did."

I walked around the rooms. They were cozy and felt warm, the furniture and the small little decorations. Finally, Peter offered me to sit near a big table in the middle of the room. Peter's mom had already cooked a dinner. It was a wonderful steak with some vegetables, and it looked really great.

Peter's mom gave me a warm smile. "You know, you are the first girl Peter has ever brought home?"

"No I didn't know that."

"He must be really into you," she said, adding a wink.

"Mom, please."

"We don't have a lot guests, so can I enjoy same friendly chat."

"OK mom, just don't tell all those stories," Peter said, flushing with embarrassment.

"Oooh, now I will really tell. You know that one day I got a call from school. It turns out that Peter with a few friends was running all around the school like crazy, he even bumped into the principal, so they called and explained that I needed to calm my son. And this other time he got into a fight with some boy, because of a girl and accidentally broke the vase in school. After that they both ran to the nearest pottery shop and bought a new vase. And as I remember then they became best friends. Can you believe that? They still are friends; his name is Robert. I think. Correct me if I'm wrong, Peter?"

"Yes mom, you are right as always," Peter answered affirmatively.

"Peter seems a little wild, but he has a good heart," his mom added.

"I think I feel that," I answered.

"Did you know he wants to enlist into the army?"

"No, I didn't know that, but my brother was in the military academy."

"What does he do now?" asked Peter's mom.

"He is an explorer."

"He doesn't have a family, does he?" she asked.

"No, he's always traveling in distant star systems."

Turning a bit serious, Peter's mom turned to him and asked, "So Peter, do you want family or adventures?"

"Mom, you are asking that for the hundredth time."

"I don't want to get inside your head, but I would like to hold my grandkids someday, and I don't want to lose you. I already lost my husband."

Turning to me now, Peter said, "My father was a space pilot; he died a few years ago in combat near the Prima 363 colonies."

"Yes, he was a great pilot and an amazing person, but we always missed him when he went on those distant missions. They kept me up at nights," added Peter's mom.

While we ate the dinner, Peter's mom told her love story. How she met her husband and how they fell in love. How they wanted to live in a peaceful place, how they built their house. How Peter was born. She didn't speak about the missions anymore, she told us only about the wonderful moments that they all three had together. It was amazing to hear all the jokes and troubles that Peter got into. It made me feel close to him.

After dinner, she suggested that we look around, "Show her the house, Peter."

"Do you want to see the house?" he asked.

"Yes of course."

We went up to the second floor.

"This is my room."

It was full of all sorts of equipment and gadgets, there was a small robot on the desk, and it looked unfinished.

"What is this?"

"It just my little project. In fact, all of those things lying around here are my small projects. I started to fix everything when I was little; father was away, so I started working on the equipment, from water pumps to computers and robots. I guess I wanted to help mom somehow. This was probably the best way to do it."

"So you fix everything around the house?"

"Yes I guess so, a few things are harder. I still can't make one farm bot work; it just doesn't seem to budge."

"Can I see it?"

"OK, it's in the barn."

In the barn I saw a rusty old robot with lots of wires hooked into a computer.

"Did you run the diagnostics?"

"Yes, it doesn't show anything. Every test comes back OK. I have no more ideas."

"Where did you get the diagnostic tool?"

"From the globalnet of course."

"What company is this robot?"

"iKoon."

"I see. Did you know they cut support for old models long time ago? It's a policy to get people to buy new ones."

"So where should I get the diagnostic tools?"

"My father has a few; we use them on our bots. I will send you some programs. Hopefully, they will work for you."

"Thanks."

"Don't mention it."

So we walked around his farm, and he showed me around, there were a few horses.

"You raise horses?"

"A few, we just like having a few horses around."

"I love horses. Can you take me for a ride?"

"Sure."

Peter put me on one of the horses and climbed onto another one himself.

"Just hold on and let's go for a walk."

We were riding the horses into the open fields. These were beautiful fields with endless yellow flowers. It was amazing.

"Can we stop? It's so beautiful."

Peter came up next to me on the horse and kissed me very gently on the lips.

"That was wonderful. Can you do it again?"

He leaned his head and gave me a passionate kiss. I felt like I was in the clouds.

When we returned home, I loved him even more. He showed me beauty and passion, and I was sure I would never forget this day.

Peter offered me a ride home. When I finally got back, dad was sitting on the couch and talking to mom. They were just talking, for once they looked happy. It felt good to see how the parents got closer. They weren't arguing over anything for once. I came closer to them.

"Hello, I see you both are getting along."

"We are remembering our young days; we remember how we fell in love. It was a beautiful day in July," reflected my father.

"It was June, darling," quipped Mom.

"Sorry my love, that was so long ago."

"Don't worry, just tell the story."

"Well, the first time I saw her, she was riding a gravibike, and she nearly ran over me."

"You were daydreaming and I was in a hurry, and I was late for my anatomy class."

"When she stopped, I looked into her eyes, and I realized I had never seen anything more beautiful than that."

"I was in a hurry and late, but your father seemed nice and when he offered me to have a tea with him, I just skipped class for that day."

"Yes, and you always complained to me about it. Because I was the reason why you nearly failed the anatomy exam."

"But that was the truth. That class was really important. The main question from the exam was from that class I missed."

"But you didn't fail."

"I was just lucky, but I'm even luckier to have such a beautiful family. Come on over here both of you."

My father came closer to my mom, they both hugged, and I came and hugged them both. It was wonderful. I felt alive and closer to my family than ever before. I loved them both and felt happy for them. I loved the whole world in that moment. I couldn't be happier. We sat down and talked. We talked about everything that bothered us, made jokes, and we were just happy. I told them about Peter, and they both seemed joyful. They accepted him and wanted to meet him in person. Later, Max called.

"Hey sis."

"Hello, brother."

"How are you?"

"I'm great thanks."

"You know there will be a big announcement about our discovery in the news. You can watch it later tomorrow. It will be the biggest thing in the news, don't miss it OK?"

"Yes, I would not miss it for anything in the world. I love you, Max.

"I love you too sis, see you on the big screen."

Max finally made it, the life for me and my family was going better than I could ever imagine. It was a wonderful day. I told father about Max, and he said that he would finally open that big bottle of wine, that he kept for a very special occasion—he was happy. I could see it in his eyes. He was proud of both of us. He was glad that I was doing great in school. He was happy to hear I met a decent guy like Peter, and most of all he was proud of his son who made the biggest discovery he ever could have imagined.

Next day, I met Peter.

"How are you today?" I asked him.

"I'm great thanks. How are you? You look really shining.

"Thanks. I want to invite you to my home. My family wants to see you," I said with excitement.

"OK great I will be there. When should I come?"

"Five o'clock will be fine."

"OK see you there," he said, before adding, "by the way, you look beautiful today; your eyes are just sparkling."

"Thank you, see you later."

I couldn't concentrate in school; the anticipation for this evening was just building up. When I got home, I helped my mom cook the dinner and prepare the table. I was so nervous. It was a big day.

Finally, the doorbell rang, and Peter was here. He had a vase with beautiful red flowers in it. I had never seen these flowers.

"It's for you. I hope you can grow them in your garden; I wanted you to have live flowers, because you are real and filled with energy."

Father invited Peter to come in. Peter looked a little nervous, because of my father, but somehow they seemed to get along just fine.

We all sat down at the table.

"So Peter, what do you do in life?" my father asked.

"I'm just studying and helping my mom around the farm a little."

"So what kind of jobs do you do?"

"Fix the machinery; fix the farm bots, all sorts of mechanical and farm stuff."

"So, you are really busy. How is the school?"

"I'm no genius, but I get pretty decent grades."

"What are you thinking about doing in the future?"

"Sometimes I think I want to be a soldier like my father, but I like working on a farm too."

"Where is your father?"

"He died in one of the conflicts on the outer rim near the Prima 363 colonies. He was a space pilot."

"Does your mom approve of you wanting to be a soldier?"

"No, she is very upset about it."

"I can't blame her. She lost her husband, and she doesn't want to lose her son as well."

Everybody somehow became quiet. The air in the room was still.

Mom broke the intense back and forth that had been going on between Peter and my dad. "OK let's eat. We have a wonderful dinner today. It's potato salad with some roasted beef."

"It looks wonderful mom," I said.

"Come on kids, dig in."

"It's really good," I complimented.

"Yes, Miss Jameson it's wonderful," added Peter.

It was a wonderful dinner, father told fun stories about his youth, and Peter added some of his own. Mom was cheerful, after all that time she seemed happy.

Dad turned on the holoTV. It was broadcasted through all the channels. They showed a team of scientists and explorers. My brother was standing next to the head of the exploration team.

"Is it starting already?" I asked.

"What is?" asked Peter.

A man who appeared to be the head of the exploration team began to speak, "Today we have made the biggest discovery since the discovery of fire. We found ruins, which date back further than our own known history. Their origin is unknown, but they clearly suggest that we are not alone in the universe. The energy signatures of this place are beyond our imagination, how it was powered and how it contained such portions of energy is unknown. However, we think we found a key. There is a small crystal that could contain all the information about the owners of these ruins and maybe a way to reach them. We will give all the information we have with the crystal itself to the best scientists in the world and hope that in time, we can give you more information.

"That was my son standing next to the head of the team. I'm so proud of him," my father said.

"We are all proud," added Mom, wiping away a tear of pride.

Peter added in awe, "It's wonderful. It changes everything, and it means there are other intelligent species in the universe.

"Yes, it opens new doors. I hope I live long enough to see them," I agreed.

"However, there is a danger," said Dad. "They could be very hostile."

"They must be much more advanced than us. We would apparently be more like insects to them, and they probably wouldn't even care that we exist," added Mom.

"Yes, you are probably right," agreed Dad. "Can I ask you something, Peter?"

"Yes," he said.

"Does your mom miss your dad a lot?" asked Dad.

"Yes, she cries often."

"When you have to make a choice about whether to be a soldier or not just think about your mom. Could you do that?" my dad asked with a serious expression writ across his face.

"Yes I will think about her."

"Do you love my daughter, Peter?" my father suddenly asked.

"Yes, I love her very much."

"Think about her too."

Mom suddenly broke up the serious conversation with a yawn. "It's getting late."

"OK Peter I will lead you out," I offered.

"It was nice to meet you all," Peter said with warmth in his voice.

"It was our pleasure too, Peter. I can see decent people from a distance. You're a good one, Peter. Just be yourself and don't change," said my father.

"I will, Sir."

I took Peter to his car. He seemed a little agitated.

"Are you nervous, because of my father?"

"He can see through people, but he's a good man. He wants the best for you."

I wrapped my hands around his head and kissed him.

"You are the best for me. I can feel it. I felt it the first time I saw you. The first time we kissed and the first time you wrapped your hands around me. You really love me, do you? Look me in the eyes."

Peter looked into my eyes, and he seemed much calmer. He seemed to have forgotten everything else and kissed me with intense passion. My body shivered. He started to kiss my neck. I was breathless; I felt shivers all over my body. He was amazing. His kisses made me feel complete, and I had never felt better in my life. I didn't want him to stop. He was amazing. Suddenly, something ran fast near the car. We looked. It was a rabbit. When we saw those long ears, we both laughed and smiled at each other.

"OK, it's time for me to go inside. See you tomorrow," I said.

"See you later, Evelyn. I love you."

"I love you too."

When I returned home, Dad was chatting with Mom. They were happily celebrating the wonderful day they'd had and the bottle of wine was almost empty.

"Are you having fun?" I asked.

"Yes, we are totally enjoying this day. I liked your boyfriend; he's a fine young man," said my father.

"I know. I like him a lot," I responded.

Dad patted the couch next to him and mom. "Come on sit beside me."

We all sat on the couch; dad hugged me and my mom.

"I am so happy today. It's one of the best days I've ever had. I love you both. I have a wonderful wife and a magnificent daughter. What could I ask more? My son made a discovery of a lifetime. My daughter is making smart choices in life."

"And what about me?"

"You are always shining bright in my life, and now you are shining even brighter."

I saw my mom kissing my dad, and I knew that we all were really happy. That was the best day in our lives, we all were in the best of moods, and we all wished this day would never end.

The next day I went to school cheerful and happy. I was glad that everything was just perfect for me. Peter looked happy when he saw me. He came closer leaned his head and softly kissed me. We went for a walk in the schoolyard. It was beautiful, there was much fresh air flowing by. We sat down near a tree. I could smell the fresh leaves from that tree.

"Are you happy spending time with me?" Peter asked.

"Yes, you are a wonderful person; I like being with you."

Peter leaned his head and kissed me on the upper lip. I felt happy to know that he cared for me. I could tell he was the man I would like to spend more time with.

"Have you ever climbed a tree?" he asked suddenly.

"No I haven't."

"Would you like to visit a place I know of? It's a lot of fun and a good way to exercise."

"OK where are you thinking to take me?"

"There is an amusing place near here, you can relax and just have fun, and there are lots of people who gather there, there are attractions, carnivals and just entertaining stuff."

"All right I would like to see that place," I said.

"Fine we can go there tomorrow. I will take Anne, Josh, and Robert too. It will be fun for all of us."

"OK, see you tomorrow." I kissed him goodbye and went to my class.

I was very excited for tomorrow; my head was just spinning about the stuff that could be there, what fun we could have. What adventures we would go through together. I was a bit anxious. However, classes were fine. I was studying hard and the physics lab went pretty well. There was an experiment of dispersion. We took a dispersive prism and light coming through that prism caused different colors to refract at unusual angles, splitting white light into a rainbow. My lab mate was a smart guy, so we finished it pretty quickly.

When I returned home, my parents seemed happy, they both looked like they were in love again after many years of hidden feelings and fights with each other. I guess this is how love goes, when you love someone really hard you get angry at them sometimes. You want them to be better or even argue for the smallest of things, just to show that you care. I loved my parents, and I seemed to understand them. They really worked hard for Max and me to become the people who we are today, and they are just happy for what they see in us. They always wanted us to grow up to be better people, every victory we achieved inspired them and every failure broke their hearts. Every parent wants their child to have a better life than they did.

I went upstairs to talk to my brother on the net.

"Hello, Max."

"Hello sis."

"So what are you up to right now TV star?"

"Remember that giant ship 'Independence'?"

"Yes, I do."

"Then guess where I got assigned to?"

"No way, really?"

"I'm on it right now."

"Wow, that's great, why are you there?"

"It turns out, they have a great scientific crew back there. They are bringing even more scientists and equipment on board."

"So, you're now on the ship of your dreams. I'm proud of you."

"Yes, the ship is wonderful. It's like a giant steel city, and the captain is a great guy."

"I'm glad for you.

"They assigned me to the reconnaissance team. They are great guys. They have seen a lot. We keep joking how the aliens would look like. One of the guys said it should have three boobs. The other said it will probably be little green men with antennas on their heads. One of them got us really laughing. He said if we meet the advanced life form of unknown origin it would have to be so ugly, that we even won't notice those three boobs."

"I'm glad you're having fun."

"Yes, it's lots of fun here. I feel like I'm home."

"So what else is new? Did you find somebody, or are you just running around chasing every girl on the ship?"

"As a matter of fact, I'm still running around sis. However, when you mentioned it, there is one interesting person on this ship. One young doctor seems different than all the other girls. She's more of a secret to me. I can't really understand her."

"So, you like her?

"No, I don't really."

"You are just denying it."

"Maybe I am, so what? Have you heard the news? Many AIs are really gathering somewhere in the part of unknown space. It's strange, people are reporting missing or rogue robots all over the sector. On the other hand, the riots are slowing down. People are getting their jobs back, because the lack of confidence is disappearing due to advanced and costly technology.

Companies are depending on human labor again. I think the worst is over."

"Glad to hear that. And brother, please be good to that doctor, don't be an asshole."

"OK, I will. See you, sis."

"See you, alien hunter."

"That one was good. Bye."

So, things were getting better. Even the problems on Ella were fading. I can't wait for tomorrow, interesting what Peter has prepared for me. I was very anxious and got to sleep early to relax, before tomorrow.

I woke up early and was very excited. Peter came to pick me up. He looked handsome as always. Anne, Josh, and Robert were in the car too.

Anne asked, "Are you ready, Evelyn?"

"Yes, I think I am," I answered.

Josh teased, "She doesn't know where she is rushing into."

"Don't worry, it's not life threatening," said Peter.

Josh laughed. "Maybe just a little."

Anne looked at the boys and back to me, "It's fine, we all have been through it, and we all are still alive."

After some time, we arrived at a place where people were hanging out, drinking some beers, eating some great food, having some fun on the swings, and riding down water slides to a pool. The place looked great for having fun, or just for relaxing and hanging out. The buildings were made from stone and wood with roofs made of straws. It was like a huge barn with lots of fun attractions.

Then I saw it. It was the main attraction. There were many trees with platforms and there were many wires between those platforms with all sorts of obstacles to overcome. There were plain wires to walk on; wooden stumps to walk through while holding onto the wires. It looked more like a circus show than anything that would seem like a free-time attraction. First, we got to the main kiosk where they prepared us for climbing the trees. They put some safety belts on us to keep us from falling down the trees or the cables. They secured them tightly. Then we were given brief instructions on how to climb and how to be safe when doing that. There were two security hooks that must be hooked all the time when climbing and when we had to get on to the different cable, first we have to unhook one cable while leaving the second hook hooked and hook the first hook to another cable, then while leaving the first cable hooked you must unhook the second one and hook it to the other cable. The main purpose of the hooks was that we always had to have one cable always secured, if something would happen. Security first, as the instructor said. Then there was a third device, it was used to slide down the cable. It had to be put on the cable, and with two safety cables and the sliding cable secured you so you could slide down. Now we had to try everything ourselves. We climbed on the platforms one by one. Peter was first on. He climbed the first obstacle very easily. Robert followed him, and he was doing it even more easily. Then I wanted to be next. It seemed hard at first. The obstacles seemed to swing, and you had to have good coordination, but I came through. The second one was harder. It had a few small wooden stumps joined together with a wire. It seemed like I had to go through the timber stumps while floating in the air. The next one was even more interesting. It had wooden sticks on lines, which were sliding backward and forward. It felt really scary, because you have to move from one stick to another, and it wasn't truly easy at all. Then it was the single cable line, the attraction that made you feel like a circus acrobat. You had to hold yourself steady holding on to the two cables and walking the single cable that was truly long. I was really trying my best to balance my body and walk slowly. When I was finally through I was truly happy with myself. And then there was an extremely long way down, a cable all down the hill through the river, it looked very scary, and I was a little anxious about sliding down that cable. Peter and Robert were really enjoying that slide; they kept on cheering me up from below. I put on the two safety cables, and I put a unique sliding hook in front, then I took my one hand on top of the special hook, and the other on the safety line wrapped around my body and the sliding hook. I was really scared. It felt like my heart was going to pop, but I moved forward and was suddenly sliding down the cable. It was marvelous. I felt the adrenaline rushing through my body. I forgot all my fears and just enjoyed the moment. I could feel the wind blowing by, and that feeling of freedom from sliding down stayed with me even when I reached the end of the line. It was wonderful. I never felt better before. I hugged and passionately kissed Peter.

"Thank you. That was a wonderful experience."

"I'm glad you liked it."

"What shall we do next?"

"Maybe let's try harder obstacles and bigger slides?"

"Ok let's go. I would love that."

That day we tried every obstacle and every course in that place. There were many hard ones, the slides were longer and the obstacles were harder, even to the point you almost have to be an acrobat to get through. It was so much fun; we almost lost our sense of time. There were even more things to see and explore, like the shooting range, the sculpture park, swings of all sorts and sizes. We even tried the children's attractions like jumping on the giant air-filled balloon, it was lots of fun. Then we got into the small zoo. We saw lots of animals there running freely: a donkey, few frightened rabbits running all over the place, lots of small goats, a few lambs, exotic chickens, a couple of swans, a few scared roe-deer's and a peacock, who suddenly spread his beautiful tail—it was an amazing view. After the zoo, we went to eat. We all were tired, so we wanted our stomachs full as soon as possible. There was lots of foods to choose from: you could eat steak or sushi, something that looked like potato pancakes or Chinese food. The food variety was really wide. I wanted some sushi. Peter and Robert grabbed a large steak with French fries. Anne and Josh ordered some Chinese food, and we ordered a big tower of root beer to share. We were so tired that we ate very slowly. Everything tasted great, Peter and Robert really enjoyed their steaks. Anne and Josh loved their Chinese food, and my sushi was amazing. After that we went onto the swings, we just wanted to fool around. I sat down with Anne and Peter, and Robert and Josh pushed us as hard as they could. We were going higher and higher. It was scary, but really fun. I felt Peter grabbing not only the swings, but my waist and bottom too. I liked it; in fact, I really enjoyed his touches. We had an excellent day, when we were going back to the gravicar I ask Peter to wait; I wanted to thank him for a great spent time. He grabbed me on my waist, leaned his head closer and kissed me like he never did before—I felt butterflies all over in my stomach, I was excited beyond imagination. It was so magnificent that I almost couldn't feel my legs. He was really good. His tongue was inside my mouth, not too deep and not too soft. It felt like a dream. Afterward, we went to the gravicar. We were all laughing and making jokes. It was a good day. We all were happy, and I wanted it to last forever. When we were driving out by the open fields with no traffic, we stuck our hands out of the windows and could feel the warm summer breeze. It was like surfing in the air and wonderful like flying in the clouds. Our gravicar was open, so Peter and Robert took out an empty blanket and made it flare out like a sail as we drove home, and I never felt happier. That day my parents couldn't recognize me, I was so energetic and optimistic that they almost thought I was sick. I went to my room to relax and fell asleep right away.

In the morning, my mom tried to wake me up. It was time for school, but I couldn't even get out of the bed. I was so tired, I felt like I could sleep the whole day. Eventually, somehow I got myself to school. I was sleepy, but somehow I got to the first math class. I don't remember how it happened, but I probably fell asleep in the class, because when I woke up, I saw an angry math teacher right in front of me and the whole class laughing their heart's out. I got sent to the principal, and you guessed it. I fell asleep there too. Finally, my mom came, drove me home, got me into the bed, and then I slept the whole day. It was a pretty memorable day, and after that a month or two I could hear people in the school call me sleepy, but I knew it was all worth it because I would never forget the best day in my life and the day after.

That night I had a strange dream. Peter and I were in a big spaceship, and there were people running all around. I remember I was scared and pressed closer to Peter, but the weirdest thing was that I could hear my brother's voice shouting through the speakers and giving commands like he was a captain. That was a strange dream, my brother is a loose cannon, and he couldn't command a resource gathering vessel, let alone command a giant spaceship. That dream was really weird and woke me up. I was scared somehow, but what was I scared of? The riots had ended, there couldn't be another civil war. I was confused; maybe my mind was playing tricks on me again.

Later, I called my brother and told him about the dream.

"What do you think?

"I don't know, sis. It's unusual. I don't want to be a captain, and I'm pretty fine being on the reconnaissance team. You just had a bad dream, and that's all."

"Is there something new, what new and interesting things can you tell me?"

"There isn't much, the scientists are working really hard, but that crystal. It's something from out of this world. It contains such energy signatures that scientists don't even know where to start from."

"Is there something else?"

"The captain called me. We had an interesting chat."

"Tell me more."

"I saw a picture on his desk; it was his wife and a child. I asked how his family doing. Captain's face just changed; suddenly, he became a different man. He told that his family was killed, because of him, because of his work, he didn't tell any details. Then he looked at me and told me that I should find something of value in this life, something more important than myself. He told me that he could tell good people right away, even if they pretend to be assholes, and that I should stop making a lot of fuss running from one place to another and become something worthy."

"Your captain is a smart man."

"Yes, he saw right through me, like looking through the glass window. I respect him. He is an honorable man."

"That's good; maybe he will teach you something. Assholes come and go, but the real people stay in other people's memories."

"Yes, sis, I will probably have to change my attitude. OK see you later, have a good day."

I liked that my brother told me that, and I felt like he really wanted to change. Maybe his work on that ship would be good for him.

The next day I drove to school. I was thirsty, so I went to the fountain. I just wanted a sip of the water, and suddenly somebody started to tickle me. I turned around. It was Peter.

"How are you doing beautiful?"

"Thanks, I'm great," I said.

"Will you sleep through the class today?"

"Ha ha, really funny."

"Everybody is calling you 'sleepy head,' it's funny."

"I fell asleep in one class." I groaned in embarrassment.

"And in the principal's office, I hear," Peter added.

"How do you know about that?"

"Everybody knows."

"I'm so embarrassed."

"Don't be, everybody will remember you, even when you finish the school."

"That's not the way I want to be remembered."

"What's the difference? The important thing is that they will remember you."

"Maybe you are right."

He leaned forward slowly and kissed my upper lip, then he went for my lower lip. He was gentle, and I could even feel the kiss on the ends of my toes, it was exciting.

"Want to go somewhere after school?"

"Yes, that would be great."

I went to my classes. They were not boring. They even were kind of fun, but I couldn't forget Peter's kiss. I was daydreaming about him the whole day. I was doing well in classes, even good in English test, but Peter was always in my mind. Finally, when the last bell rang I got outside, and there he was, with his bright smile and his strong figure.

"Come on let's go."

I sat in his gravicar, and we drove off. We were driving for hours, but we finally reached our destination. There was a place to leave a car. Near our car parking place, I saw the sea. It was wonderful, there was a high cliff and all the way down there was a big and a beautiful beach. There were no people around. Peter sat down on the cliff and asked me to sit with him.

"Isn't it pretty?"

"Yes, the sea is beautiful; I could see it all from this place."

"I come here from time to time. This helps me to forget."

"Forget what?" I asked quietly.

"Father's death."

"The first time I knew he was dead. I came here. I saw this wonderful place, and it helped me to relax, then I came here another time and another. Somehow this place sets me straight. It keeps me together."

"Yes, it's really wonderful; I also can feel the warm wind and see the open horizon. This place is amazing."

He took my hand, and we walked near a big tree. I stood next to the tree. He leaned his head, gently kissed my lips. Then his lips reached my neck. He started slowly kissing my neck. I felt excited. He really knew what to do, he wasn't rushing. He was just exploring my neck. Later, he got to my shoulders. I was feeling really hot. I wanted more. Then he got to my lips again. We were in each other's mouths. We were playing with our tongues. I felt wonderful. I could do this all day long. If he wanted I very likely would have given in to him at that moment, I was in the clouds, and he probably could do anything to me. Then he just looked into my eyes, smiled, and said that I was beautiful. It was magnificent. He was magnificent, and the day was wonderful. I looked into the sea, and it looked endless, such a big horizon, such a testimony to the beauty of nature. I never saw that on Ella. I wanted to stay there forever. Peter opened his heart, he told me about his father and that brought us even closer, I really want to be with him forever. He just made me tick.

"Do you want to go home?" he asked.

"Not yet. I want to be with you more."

"OK, we can stay here a little longer. I will get you a blanket."

He brought a blanket, wrapped me in it and sat close. I felt warm and happy. He was the reason for my happiness, and I never want to let him go. I wanted for the moment to last forever, such a beautiful view, such warm feelings, such an amazing person close. Everything was perfect. We sat there for a while, looking into the waves crashing into the shore, the seagulls flying, the endless horizon, and the sun setting down. It was this moment, this view, and this atmosphere that I would like to feel time and time again. I was so happy now that I even forgot myself, the only thing I felt was the endless happiness and love for life. When it was getting dark, I saw Peter looking into my eyes.

"Why are you looking into my eyes?" I asked.

"Because they are beautiful," he answered.

"Nobody has told me that before."

"Really, you have pretty eyes. I haven't noticed that earlier."

"Why do you think they are beautiful?"

"They are deep; they seem like the ocean."

"I like your eyes too, your beautiful blue eyes."

He held me tighter and kissed my lips. The kiss was soft and gentle; he was not rushing it. I was enjoying the slow and gentle touches of his lips. I pressed closer to his body, and we stayed that way for some time. It was a wonderfully spent time. I enjoyed being with him. He made me feel safe and calm.

After the sun set, we drove back home. I felt good, because he told me important things and personal things about himself. When a man is open, that makes a girl feel comfortable. When I got home, he kissed me goodbye, and I went to sleep. It was a calm night. I slept well. My parents seemed closer to each other too. My brother was getting smarter somehow, and everything was wonderful. I was happy. I felt peace in my heart. Everything was in the right places, even better than I could imagine. I wanted to go out into the open fields and scream as loud as I could that "I'm the happiest person in the world," and it would be the truth. Many people don't realize, but it's the small things that count, not the fame and fortune, not the positions of power and an endless list of followers. The most important things are the health and happiness of your family, the loyalty of your friends, and the love of the ones that are important to you.

I was filled with energy the next day; I was cheerful, kissed my mom and dad goodbye. I went to the school all tidy and in the best of moods. I met Anne and Josh.

Anne said, "You look different today."

"Thanks, what's different about me?" I asked.

"You're in a very good mood," she said.

Josh chimed in, "Yes, you seem really happy. What happened?"

"I'm just happy about my life. Everything is going great."

"Is Peter the reason?" asked Anne.

"He and other things," I answered honestly.

"Wow, we are happy for you," said Anne.

"Yes. Have a great day," said Josh.

"Thanks, I will."

When I was going through the corridor, I saw Peter. I ran to him, hugged him as tightly as I could and kissed him.

"You're different today."

"I'm just happy."

"That's great. I like the new you." He smiled at me.

"I like me too."

"Shall we go to eat something?" he asked.

"Yes sure, today is Asian day. They are giving sushi," I said.

"Great I love sushi," he answered.

"Me too."

We went to the cafeteria. We picked the priciest sushi we could find and ate the whole thing while laughing and making fools of one another. It was great. Peter wondered why I was so happy, so I told him everything about the family, about my brother, and about how our relationship made me feel. He smiled, took my hand, and it felt really good. The classes had ended, so we went outside, we saw Anne, Josh, and Robert. They wanted to go somewhere.

Josh looked like he had an idea. "OK, we should go somewhere fun."

"Yes. I know just the right place. We will have lots of fun," said Anne.

We drove with Peter's gravicar somewhere in the direction of the sea. There was a small town, and the town was full of people, mostly tourists. We rented some tiny cars that actually worked as bikes; we had to peddle all the time. We rented two. Josh, Anne, and Robert were peddling on one, and I was with Peter. There were lots of people, but we started to race. Anne, Josh, and Robert were at the front first, but then we gained speed and overtook them. It was really fun. We shouted at each other like: get out of the way, faster captain slow and so on. It was a lot of fun. We reached a pretty place. It was a large garden, probably left by some monarch, and there were lots of beautiful flowers, statues, and a big mansion. We all walked into the garden, where we could see all sorts of flowers, from all parts of the world and some were even not from our world. We saw a lake; there were lots of ducks and a few swans. We had some bread, so we fed the ducks, swans were more careful, but eventually they came closer. Peter gave me some bread, and one of the swans started eating from my hand. It was amazing. The swan was so white and beautiful that I couldn't keep my eyes off it. We walked around the garden some more, took some photos. The day was great, sunny and warm, with a light wind. We got into the mansion. It felt really old, there were lots of paintings, statues, clocks, weapons. Everything was antique, and it felt like an echo from the past. I never could imagine that I would see things like that; we never had such things on Ella, just skyscrapers and people. It felt like walking into a fairy tale. I imagined myself like royalty in that mansion, walking through the big halls with antique paintings and old furniture it seemed so great. There was also a room full of amber jewelry and other sorts of ambers. There were many old necklaces of amber, old bracelets, hairpins, even paintings. Things that caught my eye were pieces of amber with some sort of insects stuck into them and frozen in time. I saw a very beautiful piece of amber with a bee trapped inside. It caught my eye, and I couldn't stop looking at it, then Peter came.

"Hey there. Let's go see more stuff."

"OK, let's go."

However, somehow the picture of the bee stuck in that amber remained in my mind, it was something that was amazing for me. We went outside of the mansion. There was a wedding ceremony, the bride was really beautiful and the groom looked nice too. They seemed truly happy; their friends were close by when they were taking photos. The photographer got some really good shots near the mansion and in the garden. Then I saw two white horses, the groom and the bride were put on the horses and took photos. It was truly beautiful; they would have really great memories of their wedding. They looked happy. They were really in love, I could tell that straight away, it was written all over their faces, how they looked at each other, how they kissed and everything else. At that moment, I wanted for me and Peter to be like that, so much in love, so happy and so into each other. Peter came closer to me and put his hands around my waist. I felt joyful because he was close. When the groom and the bride stepped off the horses, they just started hugging and kissing each other. For them, everything just seemed natural. They were made for each other; I couldn't stop looking at how easy it was for them to enjoy life. They were the perfect couple; hopefully, I will get there with Peter. Anne and Josh just danced with the friends of the groom and the bride. They were really having fun. Ann and Josh invited us to dance too. I wasn't a great dancer, but somehow I was pretty good, and Peter wasn't bad either, in fact, he was almost a pro. I was really surprised. We all laughed and had a great time. When we got tired, we all found a good place to rest and collapsed onto the soft grass. We looked at the clouds and started naming them. One looked like a bear, another like an elephant; Peter saw a cloud that looked like a baby.

"Evelyn, do you want kids?"

"I love kids. I would really like to have them."

"Then I chose the right person."

Peter smiled and kissed me softly. It was wonderful. The day was great. We all looked up to the clouds. We all were tired, and we couldn't move. We had so much fun that we forgot our sense of time. In fact, we forgot about everything in the world. The five of us lying on that grass were all in a great mood. I think that was one of the best days of my life, I had my friends close by, and I had Peter. Everything was right. Everything just really turned out natural, like water flowing in a river. It was a very clear and a beautiful day. I couldn't imagine it better. When we were driving home, I pressed closer to Peter; I felt safe and happy, and I almost fell asleep. When we got home, I kissed Peter goodbye and went to my room. My parents were sitting close to each other, and my father had his arm around my mother.

"How was your day?" my dad asked.

"It was wonderful, dad, thank you."

"Great for you," Dad said. "Your brother called, he asked for you."

"OK, I will call him back."

I got to my room, fell on the bed and called Max.

"Hello brother, how's the day?"

"Hi, sis, it's wonderful. Remember that good-looking doctor I talked to you about?"

"Yes, I remember."

"I asked her on a date.

"That's wonderful; you actually invited someone for a date. Good for you."

"Yes, I did."

"And what did she say."

"She said that she would think about it."

"That's good, she didn't say no after all."

"Yeah, I guess."

"OK, next time when you ask her, put on something nice and fix your hair."

"Thanks, sis. That's a good idea."

"I would like to have a doctor in our family, so don't screw up."

"OK, I will."

"Great brother, it seems we have an understanding. See you later. I see you are changing already, keep up the good work."

My brother asked somebody on a date. The last time he did that was probably in the middle ages. I hardly believe that, but maybe he actually wants to change. As I remember his longest dates lasted 20 minutes, sometimes an hour, after that it ended up in a bed. I know that because he used to brag a lot: she's blond, she's dark-haired. She's into rock music. She's a model. She's dark-skinned. She's Asian. She has 3D tattoos. She owns a spaceship, or she has big boobs or a nice butt. It felt as I really seemed interested in his accomplishments. Yeah, right. First, I was angry at him, but then I stopped caring. Now he seems different. Hopefully he's changed, and if he's not, I will personally throw him out of the airlock, because I'm really starting to like this doctor girl.

The next day I went to my class. We learned lots of things, mostly interesting ones about nature. Everybody had their place in the food chain, and everyone was useful. The soil provides minerals to the plants. The plants use chlorophyll in photosynthesis to produce oxygen. The herbivores breathe air and eat plants. The predators eat the herbivores, and when the animals and plants die, they return to the soil, and the earth gets the minerals to start the cycle all over again. The circle of life. I was interested in ants and bees. They seemed really organized, almost the same as humans. They had a queen (their mother) to lead them and give them commands. Even Einstein once said that if the bees died, people would disappear from this planet after four days. I liked the lesson. Everything in this world seemed in order, everything had its place and nature was beautiful and really powerful. It had everything that we need: air, water, food. I understood this, and it made me feel needed. It made me feel useful in the world, like everyone has its place, and I had my place too. Our planet was a beautiful place to live in, a place we all could call home. After all, Earth is the cradle of the whole human civilization.

The lesson was important to me. I wanted to help my father more. Peter would come to help too, and it was great to see my father and Peter got along so great. They felt like good friends, and I loved that, they were two of my most loved men. OK, make that three. My brother was out there somewhere in deep space, searching for something unknown, and hopefully he was changing his attitude to better. My mom started to act differently too. She complained less and did more. I called my brother that evening.

"Hello, brother."

"Hello, sis."

"How are you doing?"

"I'm good thanks."

"How are things with the nice doctor?"

"We went on a date."

"On a date, that's great. How did it go?"

"It was good. She was really smart; I truly enjoyed talking to her."

"That's great, you are changing and how did the date end."

"I kissed her goodbye and went to my quarters."

"I'm happy for you. You should date her more."

"Of course, she seems fine. I would like to get to know her more."

At last, my brother went on an actual date, and he's finally changing. Perhaps everything would be better soon; maybe my brother would finally see what's important in life. I can breathe fresh air every single day. I have a wonderful family. I have a home to come back to. I have food and water on my table every single day, and I have Peter. My life is wonderful. I couldn't be any happier. I had a delightful day today, and hopefully everything would continue to go fine.

The next day at school I met Peter, he looked wonderful as always.

"Next weekend, we are going camping with friends; it will be great, would you like to join us?"

"Sure. I would like that. Where we will go?"

"There's a beautiful place nearby, we can go there on gravibikes and put a small campsite there."

"It sounds great. I could bring some of my friends too.

"Sure. I think they all will get along just fine."

I was really sleepy in math the next morning. I thought about the camping trip that Peter brought up into my head. Peter is dreamy and I really want to be with him, I met him with his friends the next day.

"Are you all prepared for camping?" asked Peter.

"I've never been camping," I answered honestly.

"That's not a problem. Just stick with us. Has everybody got their gear?" Peter asked.

"Yes, we got our gear and a few tents," said Anne.

"I haven't got a tent," I said.

"Don't worry," Peter said. "We can share one."

"That's great and where we will camp?" I asked.

Robert cut in, "Probably somewhere near the water."

"Can you be more specific?" I asked.

"We are going to drive with gravibikes to the lake not far away. I can show it to you on my smartphone. Here you go." Peter handed me his smartphone with the map showing a blue lake.

"I see it's not far at all. Do all of you have gravibikes?"

Anne laughed. "Of course. Gravibikes are fun."

"And more exercise," Pete added.

Josh nodded in agreement. "I agree, gravibikes are great."

"Furthermore," added Anne, "we can see more of the wonderful view."

"OK, we shall stick with gravibikes," confirmed Peter.

"Yes. I agree," said Robert

"Yes, that's great." Anne said, smiling in excitement.

Josh kissed Anne softly. She seemed pleased and in love.

Josh let go of Anne and got back to planning the trip. "OK guys we have to go, our class starts soon."

"Bye."

"See you later, I have to go too," added Robert.

Peter kissed me and went to his class. I think this camping trip will be great, and I liked Peter's friends. I would like to get know them more. I had a few more classes that day and after them I met my other friends. I saw them in the cafeteria.

"Annabel, James, do you want to go on a camping trip?" I asked.

"Where are we going?" she asked.

"It's a place nearby; I will show you on my iKoon maps," I said.

James looked at the map. "Oh, I have been here."

Annabel nodded in agreement. "Yes, it's pretty beautiful, I have been here too, the lake is really clean, and the view is amazing."

"So, you want to go?" I asked.

"Sure, why not," said James.

"I just don't want to go alone, you guys will keep me company?"

Annabel smiled. "Sure".

"Ok I have to go, my lesson has to start, see you later," said James, waving as he left.

"See you, James," said Annabel.

"See you too," said James.

"When are you going to tell him?"

"What?" asked Annabel.

"That you like him."

Annabel laughed. "Let him struggle a little."

"You are something."

"A woman has to have her secrets. Remember don't give away everything, just play a little. Life is fun, you have to enjoy it. Live a little, Evelyn, don't be always so serious."

"Ok I will. See you."

"See you sweetheart."

Next day, Peter and his friends came up to my house with their bikes. My parents were worried about me, but Peter assured them that everything would be OK.

When Annabel and James joined, we drove near the fields of corn, rye, and other different plants. We were cycling in the country and Earth was a great plantation for food around the whole sector. We were feeding lots and lots of people, after all Earth was a large farm. Peter fooled around a little; he was driving his bike without hands. I guess he was just showing off. We saw a farm full of ostriches, and we wanted to get closer to them. We went to the plasma wire. It was a special type of security for animals, it gave a little shock and you had to be careful around it. We took some grass and gave it to the ostriches. Peter and Robert thought they could ride some of the smaller ones and tried to catch them. They were running around in circles and finally caught up with a few. Our young cowboys jumped on them and looked truly amusing riding them and falling off. It all was quite entertaining. We drove further to the lake. I saw the most beautiful places: rivers, open fields, green grass. Earth was really marvelous. I liked it so much. My friends were fun, they told jokes all the way. We had to drive near the mountain. When we reached the top, we saw a steep way down. We all jumped of the bikes and went down on foot, but Peter and Robert started to fool like real jackasses. They drove down the hill on their bikes almost without brakes. When we got down they just said: What took you so long?

"Why can't you be like normal people?" I asked.

"It's fun," said Peter.

"Yes, it's fun, until you get hurt," I pouted.

We drove down the road further. I saw beautiful and clear skies, trees filled with blossoming tree buds. The whole road riding the gravibikes I felt the fresh air in my lungs. I never felt that on Ella. I also could hear the birds sing their wonderful songs of joy as they greeted the spring.

Peter came from behind and started gently tickling me. It was wonderful. I liked his touches on my waist. He honestly surprised me and then he gently kissed me on the lips. I was truly excited. It was soft and gentle, the way I wanted to be. That took my mind off everything. He was really great. We drove further. There was a forest full of lime trees and oaks. It was beautiful; I had never been in a forest before. This fresh smell of forest was mesmerizing. It was like a whole new universe. Peter came up to me.

"Now look further, behind the tree, do you see?

"What? Where?"

"Look closer near those bushes."

"Oh yes, I see. It's a deer. He's so gorgeous. Those big horns; they look great."

I wanted to get closer and have a better look, but the deer suddenly ran away.

"I have never seen real nature before, it's wonderful. We lived in a metropolitan planet, there were no trees, no nature, and we had everything imported for us from other planets. I never saw such wonders before. The fresh air in the forest is wonderful." Those smells and all that natures beauty it was amazing.

"Forests are magnificent; there are trees that can last up to 2000 years or even more. What have they seen in their lifetime? How many love stories they could tell?"

"Would they remember our story?"

Peter looked me in the eyes and slowly leaned his head towards mine. Our lips were very close. He wanted me to make my move. I rushed with impatience and kissed him. It felt dreamy. He gave me a chance to take the initiative, and it was breathtaking. I felt close to him. I felt bonded like never before, it wasn't only physical and emotional, but I felt the connection on a deeper level. I felt like we were bonded, this atmosphere, this place and him. Somehow everything had meaning. I felt stronger, more confident and more in myself and in the moment than ever before.

While driving, we saw an open place in the forest. You could see the sunshine shining through the trees in that small field covered in short grass. We set up a camp there. It was a tiny and cozy open field with a lake nearby. We were trying to make a little firepit, where we could gather around when the sun sets down. It was very still and calm. We saw a couple of swans swimming by; they both looked so white and beautiful. I'd never seen swans before. They looked like newlyweds, so white and beautiful. I pressed closer to Peter; he put his hand around my waist. I wanted to be with Peter like those swans—beautiful, charming, always together and in love forever.

Robert looked at me most of the time. I felt uncomfortable, but I guess that happens when two people are into you, but you have only a single heart. Josh and Anne were into each other most of the time, they were together for so long, but still deeply in love with each other.

"What's your secret, Anne? How are you in love for so long?"

"Well I don't know," she said. "We just complete each other. We are like two sides of a single body. The left can't do a lot without the right, and the right can't do much without the left. He's the logical, practical, realist, and I'm the emotional, dreaming, optimist. One can't exist without the other. That's just how it is."

"Evelyn, I hope one day we will be like Josh and Anne," Peter said.

"I hope so too," I answered back.

Peter and Robert went to gather firewood and after some time, we had a decent fire going. We had lots of fun around the fire. Annabel pressed closer to James; James hugged her while looking into her eyes and then kissed her. We all talked about our plans for the future, Josh and Anne told funny jokes, Robert was trying to recall a scary story about a grizzly bear hanging out inside these woods. I pressed harder to Peter and looked into his eyes. His look was mesmerizing. He leaned his head to kiss me. The atmosphere was really special. I wanted it to last forever. I sensed those wonderful feelings of joy and being complete, and all those feelings filled my whole body. We all talked a lot that evening, we told funny stories about our past, made farm jokes, and laughed at the simplest things of life, like the new music videos and movies. I loved hanging out together; it was one of the most wonderful days of my life. Boys set up camp, and all tired we fell into our tents. Josh and Anne had their own, Annabel was with James, I was with Peter, and Robert got to sleep alone. Peter kissed me slowly and then his tongue gently ended up in my mouth. I shivered. He went round my neck slowly kissing it from one place to another. It was wonderful. I felt so much passion so much love for him. He was gentle and had a soft touch. We couldn't let go of each other. After all that passion, we talked for some time. He looked me in the eyes smiling and a bit later we went to sleep.

In the morning, we packed our tents and left for our homes. Somewhere along the way, we heard a soft squealing noise. Peter and Robert got off their gravibikes and followed the noise. A few minutes later, they came back with a little puppy that looked very tired and hungry. I took the puppy into my hands; he was so small almost like a newborn baby. Who could do such a thing? Leave a small, defenseless puppy in the woods? It's horrible? We gave the puppy some water, and soon he felt much better. I took the puppy with me and decided to keep him for myself; he was so cute that I didn't want to leave him. All the time it seemed that Peter was treating me differently, he became overprotective of me. That was great at first, but later I'm started to feel a little uncomfortable.

When I returned home, I showed the new member of the family to my parents. Mother wasn't excited, but father allowed me to keep him. I bought him a small dog bed to sleep in. He was so adorable, so full of life that I couldn't take my attention from him. I played with him until I put him in his dog bed. After I fed him with some milk, he was sleeping in no time, soon after that, I fell asleep too. The next day I took him for a walk. He was wonderful. I was so happy that my father allowed me to keep him. When my new pet met Ralph, my older golden retriever, they got along just fine. Ralph seemed glad to have a new friend, and I was pleased to see them both play. I fed them both and they were both so wonderful. I just love dogs; I'm glad that I found that small little puppy, I took him into my hands and just couldn't let go. I never had seen anyone like that small little fur ball of joy, he was so sweet and so cute, I just wanted to hold him and never let go.

The next day, I went to school and was full of hopes and dreams of the bright future and wonderful things to come. I started to think of a family and how I would spend my time with Peter. How we were going to get married. How we were going to have kids. I mean lots of kids. How things were going to be wonderful and happy for both of us. How we were going to live on a farm and how we were going to grow potatoes. On the other hand, maybe we would grow something else. Potatoes are not bad, but I needed variety. We would grow corn, rye, some cows, pigs, horses, chickens, and ducks. It's going to be a big farm. My body started to feel warm, and I felt like I was going to burst when I thought about Peter. However, the next moment I had doubts, maybe he didn't really love me. Oh, how I hoped it wasn't true. How I wanted for him to be a real thing, how I wished that he would be the real thing. I was a bit tired, but the lessons where interesting, it was about open space and space travel. I remembered my brother and all his stories about space explorations and different star systems, black holes, constellations, dwarfs, and space dust. It was interesting to remember those things; I really wanted to be an explorer. To travel somewhere unknown, to see more and more of something that is beyond my imagination, to visit many planets and know different people that live on them, to see planets with sandy dunes and planets with untouched and wild nature. To be able to see a newborn star, so many things to see, so many wishes to become reality. The lesson had ended; I went outside to have a sip from the small water fountain. Then I ran into Robert.

"How is the new pet?" he asked.

"He's great! I love him, he's the most amazing dog I have ever seen, and we get along quite well."

Robert nodded. "He was quite scared when we found him; it was great that you kept him. He will be a wonderful friend."

"Yes, I can already feel that he will be a great companion."

"Do you like Peter?"

"Why do you ask?"

"I just want to know," said Robert.

Robert stood still for a few seconds.

"Yes I like Peter and I think it's obvious. Robert I have to go, my class starts?

"OK what's your class?" asked Robert.

"Biology."

"I would like to go to biology with you."

"Good, you can join me if you want."

We sat down in the biology class. Robert sat next to me. Suddenly I remembered we had a biology lab exam that day. My lab partner looked interested; I knew he liked me, so he tried to impress me with his biology skills and he did. He was real good, it looked natural for him. He just quickly used his skills to determine the frog's DNA structure in a half of an hour and figured out she had an abnormal growth in her abdomen cells. If Robert hadn't been there I would have probably failed the exam, but luckily I had a genius friend with me that day.

"Want to go out somewhere?" Robert asked.

"Sure, you helped me a lot today; I'll buy you a milkshake."

"I love milkshakes."

"OK let's go."

We found a small diner in town, there were lots of ice cream, milkshakes, smoothies, some pastry, and other wonderful snacks. We saw Peter, Josh, and Anne sitting and drinking their smoothies. I ordered some milkshakes for me and Robert and we all sat down around a single table.

"How was your day?" asked Anne.

"Great. If Robert didn't help me, I probably would have flunked my exam, I totally forgot about it."

"Robert is a genius," said Anne, "this year we all finish school and Robert will probably choose molecular biology in some fancy research university, he already got a few invitations."

"Yes. I always wanted to do that. I always liked biology," said Robert.

"Dreams really come true, Robert. You will," added Anne.

"Yes, you will do many good things for many people, just wait and see," I said.

"So how's the new pet, Evelyn?" asked Josh.

"He's great; he wants to play all the time and just keeps me cheerful."

"Three hoorays for the new member of Evelyn's family," said Josh.

Everybody cheered: "Hooray, hooray, hooray!!!"

We had a wonderful time, but we had to go home. Josh and Anne had some urgent matters and Robert needed to help with some work at home. Peter offered to take me home.

"Are you happy?" Peter asked.

"Why do you ask? How do I seem to you?"

"I think you're happy."

"Yes, I am. I have great friends, and I have..."

"What do you have?

"And I have you."

Then suddenly he gave me a passionate French kiss. It was warm and gentle. Just the way I like it. Then he gave me a ride home.

The next morning, I woke up smiling. I got up early, ate my breakfast, brushed my teeth, and kissed my father and mother.

"It's a wonderful morning. See you dad. See you mom."

My dad drove me to school. I watched the fields when I passed by, they were so wonderful, those open fields of green grass, yellow flowers, corns, rye, wheat, and of course potatoes. The beauty of nature is amazing. Everything has its place. Everything is connected. Everything is in order, and my mind seemed to wonder when I saw all that beauty around me. How my people could leave this place. It's wonderful; the steel jungles of Ella seemed so distant and lost by now, that I almost forgot them. I felt safe here. I felt serenity at last. I drive to school and then I see him, this wonderful man that keeps my heart singing and jumping like on a trampoline. I come to him from behind and cover his eyes.

"Who could that be?"

I start to giggle.

"I could recognize your hands anywhere, Evelyn."

He turned around and kissed me. I was happy. I was filled with joy. Everything was wonderful. We went to the park and sat down near the tree. Peter put his head on my legs and lay beside on the fresh grass. We just looked at each other. We smiled; I kissed him a few times.

"What do you want the most in this life, Evelyn?"

"I have everything I want. I don't need anything. I want that everything would stay the way it is. It's wonderful. I want things to stay like this forever."

"Honestly?"

"Yes, truly."

"I'm glad you are pleased with me because I'm grateful for you too."

"I want that this day would never end; I want to remember every moment of today because there is nothing more precious than this moment of my life."

"I love you."

As he said that he loved me, I suddenly felt warm. I felt butterflies all over my body, and I couldn't speak from the excitement. I just learned my head and kissed him. He was pleased too; I could see that in his eyes and his smile. We both knew a secret—we were pleased only because of who we are at this moment, and that's all that mattered. We were just happy. Then we started talking about getting our own place: big farm, good neighbors, lots of potatoes, family and kids, growing old and just spending time together. It was wonderful; it was like a picture from a dream where everything was in its place. I even skipped my English class that day. In English class, they were interpreting *ThreeMusketeers*, but I already had my three musketeers: my father, Peter, and Max, that's all I needed to know that day.

When I returned home, I was in the clouds; parents were at work, so I made dinner. It turned out pretty tasty; I took some chicken meat, sliced it into little pieces, rolled it in some fresh egg, rolled it in starch and put it in a frying pan. My meal turned out especially well. Then I prepared some fresh salad and a sauce for the chicken meat. I put in some honey and soy sauce, cooked it a little in a fry pan and viola—it was a wonderful sweet sauce. When my parents returned, they were tired. I gave them some of my tasty food.

"Mmm Evelyn, I like it. It's really good," prasied Mom.

"Yes, it's wonderful. It tastes really sweet," said Dad.

"Potatoes also taste good," I added.

"Yes, I agree."

"How was the school?" asked Mom.

"It was great"

"We are glad for you," said Dad.

"You know I called your brother; there is something different about him. He talks differently," said Mom.

"Yes, I noticed that too. Something is really different," said Dad.

"I will talk to him later, but I think he's good. Maybe he's changed," I mused.

"Your brother couldn't change; he just fools around like always," laughed Dad.

"Maybe he's different now," I considered.

Mom looked optimistic, "I really hope so."

"Mom you look pale," I noted.

"Don't worry honey, I'm just tired.

"OK, Mom, I love you."

"I love you too my sweetheart."

"I'm really happy for you, Evelyn," said my dad. "You are starting to grow before my eyes little by little, and we love you both."

I kissed my parents and went upstairs. I wanted to see my brother, so I called him.

"Hello, Max."

"Hello, sis."

"I see you have company."

"Yes this is our ship's doctor. Her name is Angela."

"Hello, Evelyn," said Angela.

"Hi there," I said with a broad smile.

"Your brother is a great person; we were just talking about your family. He's lucky to have you."

"Thanks, you are really sweet. Is my brother treating you well?"

Angela laughed, "I heard stories. He's a wild one, but he's likable enough."

"He is nice. I think you could make him a better person," I added.

Angela raised an eyebrow. "Really, you think so?

"Yes, he has a good heart, but doesn't always show it."

Angela nodded. "I noticed that."

"Hello you two. I'm still here," interrupted Max.

Angela and I: "We know."

"OK see you two later," I said.

Max and Angela said simultaneously, "Bye."

I went to sleep that day knowing that everything was going great. I never got to sleep so happy before, I was excited about tomorrow, because I will see Peter again, and it's going to be a wonderful day. I know it.

I woke up early, got downstairs, ate my breakfast, kissed my mom and dad goodbye. It was a wonderful sunny morning; I could see the sun reflecting in the lake across the road to school. I was never more excited before. I wanted to see Peter, kiss him again, and just spend more time with him. I saw him talking with Robert. I rushed in and kissed Peter. He wrapped his hands around me, and we nearly lost the sense of time. We were so into each other that nothing else mattered. It was wonderful. His kisses and his touches at this moment made me feel wanted. I didn't want it to end. I just couldn't let go of his lips; we almost couldn't be separated from each other. Our feelings were so strong that I lost the track of time. I don't believe in magic, but that moment was really magical. We just looked into each other's eyes. I don't remember how long it lasted, but I felt like the whole eternity flew by. That day we spent with each other, when I wasn't in my classes, I was with Peter, we had fun, spent time near the water fountain, sat near a big tree in the center of the schoolyard, read Romeo and Juliet together. We kissed one another, and felt warm about each other. I guess that's what love is, when time flies spending it with somebody, you love and that somebody loves you back. It's the most magical feeling in the world. Nothing can compare with love. After school, we just couldn't separate from one another, we kissed, and we laughed, and it was all magnificent, but it was time to say goodbye. Peter drove me home; I kissed him passionately and went home. That day was perfect.

When I was home, parents were watching something on a TV. They said that our own created AIs are attacking our resource collectors at some sector. That was the first time I heard of the attack of Independent Ais on people. Nobody really knew how it started, who fired the first shot, us or them. Someone said that Ais just started to attack innocent human civilians for no reason; others told that a rogue human raiding party was the first who attacked the new AI based in the unknown sector, but it didn't matter. It had begun, and it couldn't be stopped. The attacks continued. My father was watching TV more and more. I was spending more time with Peter, Robert, Anne, James, Annabel and Josh. We were riding with bicycles, going near a lake or just hanging out in the nature. Everything was wonderful; I didn't care about few ships attacking our mining weasels.

Peter was visiting my home more often, and it seemed he was getting along with my parents pretty well. I liked that my parents accepted Peter, and it seemed they like him more and more. After all, he was a great person, and my parents could tell that. He was serious most of the time, but sometimes he made everybody laugh. I loved that and my parents did too.

One weekend Peter and Robert decided to visit same lake that was really famous for its beauty somewhere near Roberts house.

We all gathered at Peter's. There were Josh, Anne, Robert, James, Annabel, Peter and me. We all were with gravibikes and backpacks. We gathered our gear and sat on the bikes. We all were in excellent moods; Peter was like a captain cheering us up. He was really in good spirits for this trip. We were riding along the open fields of green grass. You could almost smell the freshly cut grass, and it was wonderful. There were also fields full of lemon flowers, we stopped in one place and just fooled around among the giant yellow fields. It was great. There were many abandoned farms, they looked like the memories from the past, old and forgotten, but they were beautiful in their own kind of way. They were like memories that people left behind. Finally, we reached the lake. I could see a small island with a big old tree.

"Could we reach that island? I can see a beautiful tree there."

"We could if we found a boat."

Robert: Isn't that a boat?"

We all looked, and we saw it too. It was a pretty old boat, but it would fit us just fine. We all sat in. Peter and Robert were rowing.

Anne: If we sink I will kill you Robert."

Robert: If we sink, there will be nobody to kill."

We all laughed.

When we reached the island, I saw a tree. It was amazing; I never saw anything like it. It was really huge, old, but still very alive. Peter came closer to me and kissed me on the lips. I felt warmth inside my body.

This place was amazing, this tree and the whole small island looked so beautiful. It was summer, but this tree had red leaves on it. It was very old and special somehow. Then Robert called us.

Robert: Come here, I have something to show you."

We all went to see what Robert had found. It was an old rusty plate. It had something written on it: "In memory for the victims of a war that went long time ago. Let this tree symbolize the end of a horrible conflict." Now I remembered reading about those trees in a book. They were planted in many places to remind people of the war that took so many lives. I read about those trees, but it looked much bigger and older in reality. I looked to the tree; it was strong and marked the end of a huge conflict. Such big trees were a symbol of hope and dreams for all the humanity; they were a symbol of life.

We all are connected to the chain of life, and we all are responsible for our actions against the huge tree of life that gives us shelter, gives us shade and provides for us. Every living creature on this planet is a part of the tree of life. Every single being is connected. We have to understand this important fact, because life is sacred and our chase for the economic growth could be devastating for us, our ecosystems, our planets and everything in them. We must cherish what we have, because one day we might wake up and understand how much we have lost, just by chasing something we don't need. That tree was something that I will remember for a long time.

We got ourselves to the shore, and we all were hungry, so we started a small camp and gathered some wood in the fireplace. We all brought some food with us, some potatoes, shashlik (sliced meat on a point), sausages, cookies, juice, root beer and sweets. We put potatoes, shashlik and sausages above the small fireplace, and they roasted pretty fine. The meat and potatoes were freshly cooked, so we all put our teeth in the food, and it was really tasty. Then the sun sat down, and boys started to tell frightening stories about the maniac that rampaged in those woods. Those stories made us laugh more than actually scare us. Boys were doing their best, but somehow it didn't work out for them well. We began talking about other things, fun things, like the math teachers' brand new boyfriend, Joshes modern haircut, new pet dog that we found along the road and many other things. We had a wonderful time, laughed and made fun all the time. It was a great evening. Peter started tickling me. I laughed so hard and almost fell to the ground, and then he suddenly kissed me. I was excited. The kiss was really long. His tongue gently found a way inside my mouth. It was breathtaking. I played with his tongue too. We kissed like that for a few minutes, but it seemed like a lifetime. He was really good, and I felt exceptional. We both were special. We both could feel each other's bodies. It was wonderful.

Anne: Hey, you two, get a room."

"Maybe we will."

Anne: You remind me of us, when we were so much in love."

"You Aren't now?"

Anne: "Of course, we are. We just like the privacy more."

Josh kissed Anne. The kiss was really passionate and long.

Josh: "Now you see. We are so much in love like you two."

"Yes, you are. I can see that now."

We all at this moment stayed quiet after a while looking at the fire. It was really mesmerizing, the darker it got, the more beautiful looked the fire in the fireplace. We got tired talking over the plans in the future and telling fun stories, so we all got inside our tents. Peter put his hands around me and looked at me strait in the eyes. His look was truly attractive, and his blue eyes were sincerely deep. We were lying like this for some time; afterward, he kissed me gently on the lips. His kiss was really soft. Afterward, his tongue got into my mouth. We were playing with our tongues, and then Peter went around my neck. I felt like I was in the clouds, his tongue was all around my neck. I felt warmth in my belly. It was amazing. My love for him just kept on growing. His tongue made hurricanes, and he was all over my neck. I didn't want him to stop. He was doing really well, and he knew what to do. I felt hot; it was an amazing feeling. My whole body shivered. I felt his hand slowly sliding down my body. I whispered:

-I'm a virgin.

Suddenly, he backed away. He looked at my eyes like never before. I felt uncomfortable. He stopped for a moment, went with his fingers through my hair, kissed me, hugged me, looked at my eyes and just started to talk. He talked about many important things about his life, like childhood, memories of his previous love that broke his heart and left him for some guy with a new gravicar. After some time, my tension faded away. I felt calm, because he told me things about himself, he wouldn't say to anyone before. I felt little relieved. That night we didn't sleep, we talked all the time and didn't even notice that the morning had come. I looked into his beautiful blue eyes, and everything was clear. I really loved him.

We all gathered round the fireplace to talk. Peter has been in good spirits as always. He made jokes and made us laugh really hard. We all were tired, and we wanted to go home, so we packed our things, the boys gathered up the tents, and we went on a trip home. This day was great; Peter tickled me a few times. We kissed, and his smile made my day. The air was fresh and warm, there was a light breeze, and it was really refreshing. The fields looked even more beautiful on our trip back. Those fields mesmerized me, and I had never seen such beauty of nature. I asked boys to stop; I wanted to feel the fresh air.

The wind of clean air and warmth from the sun almost left me breathless. I stretched my hands and felt how the wind is gently flowing through me, the first time during my life. I felt liberated and weightless. My mind just ran loose. I was happy. I felt like I was loved and cherished. We were near a lake, so boys only took off their clothes and jumped in. I, Annabel and Anne only laughed at how they were fooling around in the water. However, after a while, boys saw us laughing, so they took some water into their hands and rushed with it in front of us. They poured the water they had in their hands at us. It was fun, we all laughed by just having a great time and fooling around. On our way home, Peter kissed me a few times. He was really good. I felt passion in him when he did that. We got near my doorstep, everybody said their goodbyes, and I finally got home.

My parents were happy to see me.

Mom quickly asked, "How did it go?"

"It was great; I really had a wonderful time."

"Good for you, what did you do?" asked Dad.

"We just spent time in nature."

"There is plenty of that here; I see you've almost forgotten Ella."

"Yes, this place is far better."

"We are happy for you honey." My mom seemed genuinely happy too.

My parents hugged me. It was a great day. I went to my bed and fell asleep right away.

The next day, I had to go to school. It was really hard to get out of the bed; I just wanted to sleep all day. But like many things in life, you have to do what you have to. I gathered my strength, got up, ate my breakfast, and went to school. I was really in a good mood, just a little sleepy. When I got into school, I saw Anne and Josh, they were talking. After some time, they noticed me.

"Hello, Evelyn," said Anne.

"Hello."

"Did you like our trip?" she questioned.

"It was great. I loved it," I answered enthusiastically.

"We should do it again," said Josh.

"Yes, I would like that." I nodded my head in agreement.

"So how are you and Peter?" Anne asked.

"We are great, thanks," I said.

Josh seemed happy for me. "Good for you," he said.

"OK. I think I will give you some space. See you later.

Anne and Josh: Bye Evelyn.

I was really happy for them. They are a great couple. I wonder. Will Peter and I turn out this way? I guess I will find out after some time. Time reveals everything. I know that Peter and I are in love, and now that's all that matters. We had a class at the gym, and one of the obstacles was climbing a rope. I got that covered already when I was climbing between trees with Peter, so I got an outstanding grade from that obstacle. Nobody really thought I would be that excellent. I guess I surprised many of my classmates. I was in pretty good shape and wanted to do more exercises, but the gym class was over, so I just changed and went into the cafeteria. Somebody came to me from behind and gently tickled me. It was Peter. I was happy to see him and kissed him on the lips. It felt good; I wanted the kiss to last longer, so I hugged him and press harder to his strong body. Later, we sat down in the cafeteria. Today was Asian day, so Peter and I grabbed some Chinese food. It tasted great, and the rice was wonderful too. We ate and talked about our previous trips. We remembered climbing on the cables between trees. We remembered how hard it was to keep steady on the cable, which was a wonderful adventure. Peter suggested that we try it again sometime. I definitely agreed. When we left the cafeteria, we saw Josh and Anne.

"Do you want to go somewhere?" Josh asked us.

"Yes. That would be great."

"Come on let's go somewhere fun," said Josh.

"OK, let's go."

We got into Josh's car and drove off. The school day was over so we could spend some quality time together. We drove near a big lake. The water was clear as glass. We jumped in. After fooling around like small kids and splashing each other with water, Peter and I got closer to each other. Peter wrapped his hands around me. I felt warmth in my body. He kissed me on the neck, and he was really good. I felt his strong hands around my body and his soft lips on my neck. It was the most wonderful thing I have ever felt. Peter was a very good kisser; I didn't want him to stop. That day was magical; I will remember everything, the gentle wind in my hair, the clear sky and the warm body of Peter beside me. I was happy. We got near the car. I pressed closer to Peter. He was the man I'd been looking for all my life. I knew he would never leave me.

Anne chimed in, "You love birds look so wonderful together."

"Thanks, Anne. You and Josh are a beautiful couple too."

She blushed, "We try our best."

"I know you do your best, but how do you make it work so long."

Anne paused before answering. "It's simple. Everything in this world needs hard work. Relationships are no exception. It takes hard work and that small wonderful ingredient called love. When you come to realize that, you will have long-lasting love."

"Thank you, now I understand."

"No need to thank me, just live your life and love the one that's close to you. That's all that you need at the end of a day. Just don't forget, strong relationships need hard work. It's harder to keep an excellent relationship than get a good grade in school or earn lots of money."

"Thanks, I will remember that."

I will remember her words. She was a really smart person. I haven't known anyone as intelligent as her before, she is an inspiration for me. She knows what she wants, and she treasures what she has. Many people don't value the things they have, and they lose everything. It's sad, but it's true. After all, everything that has value comes to those people who treasure it. Those people that don't value what they have will always lose it. The evening was really beautiful. The sun was going down, and the whole sky was red. It was a beautiful sight. I wondered how many people are looking into the sky right now, how many people are inspired by the magnificent view that I see. It's a wonderful quiet place our Earth. I love my life. I love this planet, and I love these people. I pressed harder against Peter's body. I was happy.

When we arrived home I was in the clouds, I didn't want this day to end. I couldn't let go of Peter. I just wanted him to stay with me longer. He was a very good listener. We talked for about 30 minutes, and then we hugged and kissed. It was the most wonderful evening of my life. It was sad to say goodbye, but Peter needed to go home; he had to get some work done.

Finally, I was at home. Mom and dad were near a holoTV, listening to news. I sat down closer to be with them. It was the first time I heard about it. Some drone ships attacked a mining colony in the outer sectors. The scientists informed that the drones were machine piloted ships, and they had never seen anything like it. The technology was unknown to anybody. This was something from a science fiction book. Humans couldn't create these ships. They were very advanced. It was only the beginning, the beginning of the big war between AIs and humans. I couldn't understand why such horrible things happen. Reading history I understood that we were constantly battling for something, we fought for a lump of bread, and then we fought for land, our struggles continued for resources, for dominance, for authority, for other planets and solar systems. We were constantly struggling for something, perhaps it's in our nature, and maybe we aren't destined for peace. I really hope I am wrong because only when we are at peace with ourselves do we achieve the greatest victories. We overcome our fears. We strive for greatness. We create. We love. We reach for our goals, and most importantly we live.

Father didn't talk much, but I understood that he was focused. He knew something, something that bothered him. I could feel it. I thought to myself, what could a few raider ships do, it's only a small force? One way or another, the human empire is enormous. We had huge numbers of conquered solar systems, large fleets with gigantic dreadnoughts, carriers, frigates, and fighters but my father clearly had his own opinion. He was a smart man and probably knew something that nobody was telling us on the holoTV. My father was upset. He predicted this, but he always hoped this wouldn't come about. He hoped that this war would never begin, but his hopes were slowly slipping away.

"Why are they attacking us? Don't they know that we are peaceful? Those miners didn't hurt anyone.

"I don't know. They are just machines; they don't really realize the value of life. They don't have something we call a soul or consciousness. They just want to expand and conquer. That's a big problem because someone who doesn't value life is simply a machine. The logic is working like this is good and this is bad, but such things as compassion and kindness are nowhere to be found in the logic of a machine.

I finally understood my father. He made it all clear. We were facing the strongest enemy yet. I wondered what the future would bring us and what challenges we would face. I wanted to be more like my father. I was always proud of him. He was strong, determined, smart; he constantly told the truth, even if the truth was really tough.

I didn't sleep well that night; I thought all about those poor people who lost their lives. Some of them probably were pretty young, maybe even my age.

It was hard to get up in the morning. The lack of sleep made me feel dizzy. I knew that things like those attacks on the miners made me angry, but I don't have to think about it. Maybe it's only a single incident, and it wouldn't go further. It was Sunday; the service bots were cutting the grass, so I could feel the smell of the freshly cut weeds, it was all over the yard. I laid down in the middle and just closed my eyes; it was marvelous to feel the live grassy carpet all over the place. I remember I used to dream about laying on those open fields when I was younger; it was amazing to feel that in reality. I felt totally joyful on that morning; it was a fresh new memory of happiness that sparked even a bigger love for this planet. Earth was amazing, with all its nature and all its beauty, how could we leave such a planet? It's our home, our roots; we should always remember our roots and that wonderful nature.

I felt truly happy and thought about Peter. I wanted to visit him or just say hello. I took one of the horses we had and rushed to his place. I saw him doing some work outside. I jumped off my horse, ran closer to him, and noticed him smiling; he had such a wonderful smile. I rushed near him, hugged him, and kissed him as hard as I could. His hands were all over my body. He couldn't let me go, his lips sunk into mine, and I felt a sea of emotions running through my whole body. I couldn't stop kissing him; those memories of this wonderful place, this magnificent moment couldn't escape my heart. His hands reached my butt cheeks. I was a little embarrassed, but I didn't want him to stop. This feeling of love to him made me want more. I couldn't let go of someone like him, his every touch, every breath. Every kiss was overwhelming. He was the only one who made me feel this way. I knew that this man would be my husband and at that moment I knew I wanted to have children with him and raise them on this planet, happy together forever. All I needed and wanted to be a loving wife to a wonderful husband.

"Do you love me?" I asked him intensely.

"Yes of course." He said with a grin.

"I love you too."

I kissed him on the lips as hard as I could.

"You will never leave me?"

"No, I love you," he answered simply.

"Promise me that you will never leave me, or I will disappear and never come back," I said.

"How could I leave you? I love you more than myself," he said with intense honesty.

"OK. You have to remember something. If anything happens, no matter how horrible things get, you have to be beside me. Do you promise me that?"

"I will always be with you and won't leave you. I promise that to you."

"I love you. Do you know that?" I asked him.

"Yes. I love you too."

I hugged him as hard as I could. I even felt his breath; I could feel his strong heartbeat through his shirt. This was a moment of true joy. We both were happy because we had each other, and nobody could break us apart. That moment we both felt complete, we both were in sync with each other, we both knew that this moment marked a new beginning in our relationship, and we couldn't break our promises to one another. He leaned his head to kiss me and gave me a little space to step in. I jumped right in to kiss his lips. I kissed him as strong as I could. I was tempted by his gentle lips. He ran with all his kisses over my lips. My soul just wanted to run free. He gently went around my neck. I felt his tongue all over my left side of the neck, and Peter was magnificent. He was a real master. Afterward, he slowly got onto the right side of my neck. I almost felt him spelling words. Next, he went for my earlobe. He kissed it gently. My belly felt warm, and I was beyond the clouds. His hands were all over my body. I felt the amazing sensation of feelings running through me like little lizards. I wasn't expecting it, but his hands reached my bottom. He grabbed it tightly, and I felt like I practically wanted to burst. I nearly lost myself in his kisses and hands. It was beyond my imagination. I felt totally happy, and I knew that Peter was in the clouds too. We both were in this moment; we both felt it, that universal language of love. That was the most amazing feeling ever, and it kept on holding us together, we just stayed like that, for as long as we could, silently staring into each other's eyes, looking at each other like in a mirror. We were separate but one at the same time. We were happy just to be. We didn't want gold, power, fame or luxury items. We just wanted this moment to last. In my brightest dreams, I hoped that we would marry one day, have some wonderful children, be a healthy and happy family, or just be, just live and reach our small goals step by step.

The next day was a day off, so we wanted to go somewhere nice. There was a small mall nearby, so we drove there to get some Asian food. The place was truly great, like the atmosphere and the decorations. I truly felt like we were in Asia. The waitresses with their traditional Chinese dresses looked beautiful and were really nice. The restaurant had Chinese lamps, Asian furniture, paintings, and other appropriate decorations. I could also hear the Chinese music playing. It was so calm and relaxing. I just put my head over Peter's shoulder. When we got the menu, plates in the picture looked small, but when our order came, there were huge portions; I thought we couldn't eat it all. We ordered some chicken with sweet sauce and vegetables. We also got some rice with chicken egg. We both were happy; we could relax from work at home and at school. It was our time out, when we could just enjoy the time, eat some great food, and tell some jokes to each other. I think it made us closer. We got more attached to each other. Peter kissed me a few times. I felt better. He was wonderful, and I was happy with him. I wondered, did Peter come into my life, or he was constantly with me, or at least with me in my heart. It was like I knew that I would meet him and everything would slide into its place, or perhaps he was always with me, maybe he was regularly there for me, waiting for me to grow up, to become the person I was now and just come into my life like a gift, a gift that brought me peace and harmony. Probably he was always there and would always be in my heart. Nothing made me happier to know things like that, I have gotten closer to my roots, to my parents, to my inner self and finally to Peter. That was mind-opening, I understood that the universe was linked, we are all linked somehow, we all belong, we all are needed, and we all are special, nobody is an outcast, a freak or something other, everything is a single united thought, everything is in sync.

With those thoughts, I returned home with Peter. He kissed me goodbye, and I went into my room and fell asleep. That was one of the most relaxing nights of my life, I slept like a baby. Finally, I was whole; furthermore, I knew my destiny, and Peter would be the one who I would take with me on that journey.

Next day, I came downstairs and kissed my mom and dad, grabbed a sandwich, ate my breakfast really quick and went outside. There was Peter. His smile mesmerized my quickly, and my hands ended up around his torso, and my lips gently kissed his. I was happy, and Peter was pleased too.

"You complete me," he said.

"You complete me also," I agreed.

"I want to be with you forever."

"I want the same."

"You are different from other girls I've met."

"How?"

"You are mine."

His lips gently touched me. First, he was gentle, but the kiss became more passionate. He was all over my lips, even his tongue got into the picture. It was intense. His lips were running through my neck. It was amazing. I felt shivers all over my body. He was really smooth.

After all that passion, we sat in Peter's car and drove off to the school. The morning was a gift. I could feel the warm breeze of the wind. I could smell the freshly cut grass in the morning. The sun was bright like never before, the beauty of the open fields was amazing, you could see corn, potato, rye, and wheat farmed all over the place. The farmers woke up early in the morning and were doing their work within the fields. I wave them hello and they gratefully waved me back. Suddenly, near the small forest, a roe-deer jumped out in front of our car. Right away, Peter hit on the brakes. We were lucky we didn't hit it. The deer just stood in one place, looked at us for a moment and went on his way again. We were lucky; we could really have had an accident. We both looked at each other and laughed. We were happy we didn't hit that deer. Then we continued our journey to school. Anne and Josh were there also.

"How are you guys?" greeted Anne.

"We're fine; we almost hit a roe-deer," I answered a bit shook up still.

"Oh, really, I'm pleased you're OK," said Anne.

"Thank you..." I said.

"Probably it's their mating season; we saw a few ones along the road as well.

"They are really beautiful," I said.

"Yes, they are," she agreed.

"I didn't see so much nature on Ella," I shared.

"Do you like it here Evelyn?" Josh asked.

"Yes, it's different somehow: the air is fresh, there is so much green all over the place. Everybody is planting something. Animals are running all over the place, and everyone is friendly."

Anne smiled at my description of Earth. "I'm glad you like staying with us."

"Yes, it's just something different, and I have Peter. I'm very happy."

My lessons had started. I went into a history class and the teacher told us about first astronomers, first manned flight to outer space, and the first landings on the Moon and Mars. The first hyperspace jumps to other solar systems, first settlers, and the first Galactic Republic. Many wars and conflicts went on to accomplish the first stable government in Ella and the time of peace afterward. Our planet also had a rich history too, three world wars and other smaller conflicts. It's very important to know your history because if you don't, you can't create a better future.

After class, I went into the cafeteria. Today was burger day. So we had some wonderful burgers. Peter, Robert, Josh, and Anne were sitting around one table, so I joined in.

"Hello everybody," I said, taking a seat at the table.

"Nice to see you, Evelyn," said Peter.

"We are glad to see you too," added Anne.

"How was your day?" asked Josh.

"It was great. I had a history class," I told them.

"Was it interesting?" Peter asked.

"Yes, it was very engaging. I like history, and I like biology."

Anne suggested, "So perhaps you will be a doctor some day?"

"Who knows, maybe?"

"My girlfriend is going to be a doctor. I will be very proud of you, Evelyn."

"I like to help people; it brings meaning to life somehow," I said.

"Great," exclaimed Josh, "we will have a doctor friend."

"Thank you. You are the most amazing friends whom I had."

Anne added, "Don't say had. You have us now. Don't you?"

"Yes, I mean I have."

"Come on, you haven't heard me snoring, you will be thinking otherwise when you do," laughed Josh.

"Come on, Josh," said Anne. "Cut it out."

"He snores very loud Anne. You have to admit that," added Peter.

"I love him the way he is." Anne kissed Josh on the lips. It was a long and warm kiss.

"It's a good day. Everybody is happy; we are having a great time. We should go out somewhere," said Robert.

"Yes, I agree. We really should go out," agreed Peter.

"Where could we find a nice place?"

"Let's try Boogies," suggested Peter.

"Boogies? What's that?" I asked.

"When we all are in good moods, we go to Boogies," explained Peter.

Josh added, "There are pool tables, a bowling alley, table games, arcade and tasty food."

"Don't forget the beautiful waitresses," chimed in Robert.

"How we can forget those. You dated one of them when you got 18 as I remember," reminisced Peter.

Robert frowned. "It didn't turn out as I planned."

"Yes, she left you for some rich bastard whom she met later in a bar."

Yeah, that was a long time ago."

"OK, let's forget about that and focus on having some fun. To Boogies everyone!" exclaimed Josh.

"Don't forget Annabel and James," I added.

Anne agreed, "Sure, we will pick them up."

After we picked up James and Annabel, we all got into our gravicars and drove off. Josh and Robert were driving. I pressed myself deeper against Peter's chest. He wrapped his hands around me, and it felt wonderful to be close to someone I loved.

Then I saw the place. It was a pretty old building, but it had lots of lights and a big holosign "Boogies." It looked really great. We walked in; the place was full of all kinds of people. There were street artists, some people who had enormous haircuts or pretending to be cowboys. We ordered a table and a bowling track. Peter was first to go. He got a strike from the initial run and then it was Robert's turn. He got a spare. Anne and Josh weren't so lucky at the game. James kissed Annabel softly. We ordered the biggest pizza we could find on the menu. Then it was my turn to throw a bowling ball. I got my first strike; I guess it was beginner's luck.

We played as best as we could, everyone got a few strikes. We were all happy. Then we got our pizza. It was gigantic. We all grabbed a bite. It was really tasty. When we finished pizza and had a few runs on the bowling alley, we ordered two pool tables. Josh, Anne, Anabel, and James took one table and me, Peter and Robert took another one. I wasn't a good player so Peter helped me out; he stood behind me and leaned closer to me, so he could show me how this game was played. He helped me and showed me how to aim and how to shoot. He was really close to me. It felt a little intense, but then I got used to having his body really close to me. I felt him beside me. It was a wonderful feeling. I almost forgot how to play. I felt hot being so close to him. We played a few times and then I couldn't control myself. I wanted to kiss Peter. It felt truly good. His hands were really strong. I wanted to feel his lips, as long as I could. This man made me feel wanted. He was truly good at everything he did. I couldn't stop kissing him. He held me tight, and I almost wanted to burst from excitement. His moves and his lips, everything seemed right about him. This man made me whole.

It was a great time out, but we had to return home. It was getting really late, and we had school in the morning. One way or another, we had a great time. I pressed harder to Peter when we were returning home, we kissed, and we both were happy.

When I returned to my room, I couldn't get Peter out my head—his lips and his body. He mesmerized me. I truly want to be with him more. My head was filled with emotions for Peter. I wanted to hear his voice, so I called him.

"Hello, Peter."

"Hello there."

"How are you?"

"I'm great, thanks, and how are you?" he asked..

"I'm good. I was thinking about you."

"Really, I was thinking about you too." I could sense his smile through his voice.

"That's nice."

"When I will see you?"

"Tomorrow at school."

"Yes, right. I forgot we have school."

"How silly. You even forgot that."

"You have some crazy effect on me. I forget things."

"I like that."

"Did you know that you are beautiful?"

"I'm not really that good-looking, you just say so." I could feel my cheeks flushing.

"No, I mean it. You are very pretty to me."

"I'm really not that beautiful."

"You are to me."

"Thanks. You are a good person. Good night, Peter."

"Good night, beautiful."

He really knows how to treat women. I'm truly happy to have a man like Peter. I didn't want to sleep yet, so I called my brother.

"Hello sis."

"Hello there."

"How are you?"

"I had the most wonderful day ever."

"I'm happy for you, sis."

"And how are you?"

"I'm dating that doctor now."

"That's great, you're a changed man, keep it up. Don't hurt her feelings OK?"

"I won't. I like her a lot."

"That's great; you see it's better to let somebody closer."

"Yes. She's an excellent person."

"Keep up the good work and see you later brother."

I was happy for my brother, at least now. He was getting his things in place. After all that running around, he seemed like he was doing pretty well now. After talking with Max, I couldn't get Peter out of my head. He was a single thought that I couldn't get out of my mind all night.

In the morning, I was tired because of the lack of sleep. Probably I thought about every possible scenario for me and Peter in my head. That man was rooted in my mind, I couldn't think about anything else. I thought that a future with him would bring stability and happiness in my life. I really wished that. He loved me. He wasn't selfish, and he had some plans for the future, and that was enough for me. I wanted to be with him until the end, the only thing that scared me was his desire to enlist in the military, but I hoped I could persuade him to rethink that idea. He was a wonderful person, and that was truly important to me. I wanted to spend more time close to him; I thought that he could really be mine for all of my lifetimes.

It was time for school again. It seemed like every other ordinary day, but our history teacher started a different topic. It was about the new drone warships attacking our mining colonies. The teacher spoke seriously about the dangers we could face with the machines advancing at this rate. Their technological superiority was obvious. They seemed to be growing in numbers and in strength; their need for resources was also growing rapidly. She seemed very concerned and told us that this could be a beginning of another giant power threat in the universe, and this could be a start of a big war. Everybody listened because the teacher had done very serious research and the news about the Independent AI's technological progress was obvious. She said that many robots with brand new machine cores were hijacking spaceships and traveling to the uncharted sectors to join their fellows.

"What we are seeing now is a formation of a brand new power, and if it is not stopped, we will be in an extreme difficult situation," said my history teacher.

One student asked, "What are our government leaders doing about it?"

"Now they don't see it as a threat, but later they will regret their actions," she continued. "Now we have lots of troubles within. The riots and unrest are slowing down, but we still have lots of trouble within our own bowl. On the other hand, we have no information about the new AI capabilities, their numbers, their forces, their economy or their technological level. In other words, we are blind, and we still have many of our own problems to think about something that is very far from the mighty human empire."

"But the danger is real?" I asked.

"Yes, it is," she said seriously. "We don't have an idea how strong the enemy is, we don't know what the enemy is capable of, and we don't even know how the machines think. Soon we might face an attack from nowhere or many continued attacks."

That lesson bothered me; I knew the teacher was right. I knew that we might be faced with something really big this time.

I needed to see Peter. He was outside with Robert as always. Robert had brought his pet to school. I played with his cat a little.

"She's so adorable," I said.

"She's a great pet," said Robert.

"Hopefully, the teachers don't see her," added Peter.

"They won't. Don't worry," reassured Peter.

"Somehow, when you tell me not to worry; I start to worry a lot."

"Come on Peter, Robert has a wonderful pet, just relax. We are not in a military camp. It's only school," I teased him.

"OK. I just don't want to get in trouble. I remember the flower pot sometimes," said Peter.

"And do you remember the math teacher's window?"

"We broke it accidentally," said Peter.

"Only one teacher was scared. That's all," argued Robert.

"Oh, the one you had a crush on," asked Peter.

"Robert you had a crush on a teacher?" I asked.

"Yes, she was a new teacher, and she was very pretty," replied Robert rather sheepishly.

"What was up with that window?" I asked.

"Well, I wanted to secretly throw her flowers through the window and she hated me after that."

"However, it was lots of fun anyway," laughed Peter.

"Yeah, we had lots of good days," agreed Robert.

Peter looked thoughtful. "It will be sad to leave school."

"Yes, we had great times," I agreed. "I feel like this place is my home. The teachers are great. The food is decent, and most of all I have good friends like: Anne, Josh, Annabel, James, and you guys."

Robert smiled warmly, "We are glad to have you too, Evelyn."

"I am the one who is really happy that you are here." Peter leaned down and kissed me. It was a short one, but still it made me feel good. The day was perfect, so I just wanted to return home and relax.

At home, I saw my parents glued to the holoTV screen. There were lots of explosions and different sorts of warships attacking each other. That was a new human colony being attacked by the enemy AI. The fight was rough and the people barely stood ground. Small fighters and bigger warships were attacking everything that moved. It was horrible, so many people dead, so many losses. The parents couldn't stop watching. I couldn't either. Those were some really horrible scenes. The fighters were attacking unarmed people, and they had no concern for human life. I had never seen so much terror before, it looked like a massacre. Then the transmission ended.

"It has begun," my father said.

"What has?" I asked.

"We created our own perfect enemy; I don't know how the government is going to deal with it," he said caustically.

Right after that horrible video transmission there was a government official on the screen. He claimed that those attacks wouldn't go unnoticed and even now there was a group of warships approaching that location, and they would wipe out every enemy ship they could find. The man was sweating; that's when I knew the situation was serious. I realized I was really scared. I went to sleep, but my head was full of the pictures from the attack, those innocent people, how could anyone do such a thing?

It was Saturday morning. There were some noisy ideas into my head. I wondered, did Professor Everton make machines just to do work, or he made them understand love, kindness, compassion, happiness? Did he make them understand cruelty, anger, and hate? On the other hand, did he only make them as slaves for our needs and everything else they had to find out on their own? It would be a very cruel scenario for both sides: human and machine. We could see many examples in our history, which showed us that, one way or another, freedom and self-expression came at a high price. Did the machines already understand that, did they want freedom from their masters no matter the cost in human lives? Self-conscious machines could want different goals: to live happily in symbiosis with humans, or they could want to wipe us out like an outdated smartphone, without understanding what it means to be compassionate. They could see us just as mammals driven by chemical reactions in our brains, but we have something much more to offer. We understand happiness. We feel. We cry. We achieve something that is beyond our capabilities. We strive in our lives for goals that are beyond us. We dream of happy futures. We can do something that machines never will. We know the price of loss and the price of new beginnings. The experiences we come through make us who we are; we have the potential to stand together in building a better future for man and the machine. The question is whether both sides would be willing to do that, or are we too entrenched in our own problems that we can only see each other as a threat.

I felt lonely, and I wanted to talk to somebody. I called up my brother.

"Hello, Max."

"Hi there, sis."

"Did you see it?"

"Yes, we all here wanted to join the fight, but our superiors had another mission, looks like the research done here is much more important than saving human lives."

"Be thankful that you are safe. Just spend more time with that doctor. I think she is worried about you."

"Angela is a good person; she will understand that I need to protect my people."

"Yes, she might, but first of all, she's a woman, and I think she cares about you."

"Yes, she does. You are right; she needs me now more than ever."

"You are getting smarter, brother."

"One way or another, we are pretty far from that location. We would need a lot of jumps to get there."

"There are lots of military personnel, Max. They will take care of it without you. Just do your job; you will do your part when you are needed. OK, Max, see you later."

"See you, sis."

Some part of me understood that Peter was like Max and he was probably thinking about the same things, and he wanted to go blindly into the night and blast away everything that had a cybernetic brain. I went to Peter's house. His mom was downstairs. She looked upset.

"How are you?" I asked her.

"Peter is going out of his mind," she said.

"What do you mean?"

"He wants to enlist, right now."

"I will talk to him," I said.

When I got upstairs, I saw Peter packing his bag. I walked closer to him.

"Where are you going?" I asked him.

"I'm going to enlist."

"Really, you don't care about your mother or me."

"They started it. They attacked innocent civilians, and it can't go on like that."

"No, it can't, but tell me what could you do?"

"I will kill every machine I could find."

"How you can kill a machine?"

"With a laser gun."

"It doesn't feel pain. It doesn't understand fear, and it doesn't know love. But I do. I don't want to lose you."

"I have to. Somebody has to…"

I grabbed his head, sucked into his lips and didn't let go. He grabbed my body, took his hands around me, held me up higher and put me against the wall; the kisses went on and on. He went round my neck, my shoulders. He even went for my earlobe. He was all over me, and he was so passionate, that I almost forgot how to breathe. I felt chills all over my body, and that was beyond anything. He was rough, but I liked it, and I liked it a lot. We ended up in bed. He went on kissing me. He kissed my belly. I felt warm all over, and he was a passionate man. Then I stopped him.

"Will you leave me?"

"No, why should I?"

"You are going to fight."

"Yes, but I always remember you."

"What happens if you die? I will be alone."

"I don't know."

"Think about it. Just please think about it. If not for me, think of your mother."

Peter stood there for a few minutes; afterwards he sat down on a chair and was lost for a few minutes. He understood me.

"I can't leave my mother, and I can't leave you. You two are the most important things in my life. I will not leave you. I will protect you and if those bastard machines get here, I will give everything to protect you."

"I know, Peter. I am certain about it. I know it is a hard choice for you, but it can't be different. We are far away. I saw in the news, there is a big force gathering near the AI sector. They will retaliate in a few hours now. We can watch the news."

"OK, I will take my mom, and we are going to go to your place to watch the news. I think we all should be together."

Peter went downstairs and spoke with his mother. She got dressed to go out, and we all drove to our house.

"Hello there, Peter," said my mom as we walked in the door.

"Hello, Mrs. Macintosh."

"Hello there, I see you brought a nice young lady with you Evelyn," said my father.

"Good to meet you both, Mr. and Mrs. Macintosh."

My father beckoned everyone inside, "Come in, come in everybody, you are all welcome at the table; you are all my dear guests."

"I know you all are hungry, so we made you some steak with fried potatoes."

"Potatoes again, father?" I asked.

My father tested me, "Do you remember what I said?"

"Yes. If you have potatoes..."

"...You can survive anything," he finished.

"You grow a lot of potatoes?" asked Peter.

"Yes, my father just loves those."

"I like potatoes; they taste great when properly prepared," said Peter.

The news was on. There was a lot of news about the attacks on the colonies; they kept airing footage from spaceships and from the planets themselves. The human empire fleet was closing in on that location. However, until that we could see reporters risking their lives to get the latest footage. The fighters were bombarding military and civilian targets. Everything was like from a movie. I couldn't believe it; the machine fighters just had no regard for human life. It was horrible. The more massive enemy ships even attacked the colony evacuation vessels, the people in the footage all were scared, some in panic, some trying to run away from laser fire. It was a real horror. There were lots of panic and lots of despair. Then our forces arrived. They jumped into the battle. The fleet was massive. The AI tried to pull their best, but they were outnumbered and the human military prevailed. There were cheers everywhere, people were happy, because the enemy was defeated, the AI was put down. That was a wonderful moment. However, it wasn't the end. New and a lot stronger machine forces rushed out of nowhere into the battle. They were much tougher than the previous one. The battle went on for hours. Lasers were firing from every side. Ships were split in half. Fighters were everywhere, and capital ships were ramming the smaller AI battleships. Machine ships were tinier, but very efficient; they were swift, but with powerful shield technologies. The battle went on and on. The machines even sent in a few capital ships, bringing down our huge military dreadnoughts. However, with heavy losses, the human empire prevailed. The enemy backed down.

"Let's take a minute for those who died today," I said quietly.

"You are right, Evelyn; it's not only a victory, but a tragedy too."

"Yes," said my mother, "it's a great sorrow; let's take a minute for those poor souls."

We sat down for a quiet minute. Everyone in the room just stayed still. It was one of those moments when we all could even hear was each other's breath, it was a respect for the dead ones on that day, and hopefully that day wouldn't be repeated.

After the minute passed, we talked for some time and later Peter and his mom decided it's time to go home.

Peter kissed me goodbye.

"Bye, Evelyn, see you later."

"See you, Peter."

After saying our goodbyes,I helped my mom and dad to clean up. It seems they liked Peter more and more.

"Peter seems like a good person.

"He is wonderful dad.

Mother: His mom is also a good person. It seems you are lucky.

"Thank you both for the support.

I kissed my mom and dad and went upstairs. I called Max.

"Hello, sis."

"Hi there, bro."

"Did you see it?

"Yes, we watched the news all the time."

"Something tells me, we haven't seen everything yet."

"Why do you think so?"

"It seems they have no idea what they were doing. It's not typical for a machine."

"What do you mean?"

"Machines are methodical. This attack seemed different."

"How?"

"The forces were attacking randomly, picking up loose targets. The fight was chaotic. A machine doesn't do that; it's methodical, attacking targets one by one."

"You mean?"

"This was only a test. We will see more attacks later."

"Yes, probably, you could be right."

"I really hope I'm not."

"I hope so too."

"Goodbye sis. Talk to you later."

"I will bye."

I got to my bed. I felt a little worried and scared. The AI army seemed really scary to me. They were dangerous, and we were the ones who created them. Sometimes I was scared by the human imagination.

It can be so destructive. We have lots of strength, but we often use it the way that we shouldn't and this time is one of them.

I remembered Peter; I remembered his eyes, his voice. Everything was right with him. I was lucky, and I knew that I should cherish that. I knew that he was important to me.

When I got back to school next day, I ran into Robert.

"Hi there, Evelyn," he said.

"Hello, Robert."

"How are you?" he asked.

"Great just finished my biology lesson. It was quite interesting. We talked about human anatomy."

"Really," he said, "that's my favorite subject. I'm thinking of becoming a surgeon some day."

"Great, I also want to be a doctor and maybe a surgeon. We will be colleagues then."

"Yes, we could be. I'm looking forward to that. I hope we will be great friends."

"We are good friends already, Robert."

"OK, see you soon."

"See you."

It was a good day. The lessons were fun, and I saw Peter for a few times. We were happy. Everything was fine. After all the fighting far away, our lives seemed to return to normal. I remembered a quote from a well-known professor: "Where there is life, there is hope." Those were meaningful words; they meant that life is precious. It seemed that, life is hope by itself. Interesting, do machines understand that, or do they even could understand that? Life is so fragile, nothing else in this universe is like that, life is exceptional, and it must be cherished.

I went for a walk. The day was good, and the weather was warm with a light breeze. I looked through the trees. They were magnificent, those strong, high and magical oak trees, there was something about them. They were mesmerizing. I remembered Peter. He was like one of those trees: strong, determined, and stable. It looked like I finally found something that mattered, something destined just for me and something that would last. All those empty years just faded away like the smell of grass in the morning. I was really happy to be in this place, at this time, with this person on my mind. Everything else just didn't matter.

Then I saw him. He was standing near one of the oak trees. He smiled at me. I walked closer to him.

"You went for a walk?" he asked.

"I just took some free time."

"Me too."

"Do you like those trees?" I asked.

"Yes, I feel something when I'm here. It's like I'm home. Those trees must have this effect."

"Yes, I know what you mean," I said, looking deeply into his eyes.

He leaned his head and kissed me. We both were into each other's lips; we were sunk in each other. He gently went for my neck. His lips were like fresh water on my neck, and he was amazing. He went from one side from the neck to the other; his kisses were slow and passionate. Those moments under that strong oak tree, I will never forget that. Peter was really into me. He was using my neck as his own playground, then he went for my earlobe. I felt shivers all over my body. I wanted to be like this forever, but Peter stopped.

"Would you like to see something?"

"Yes."

"Come on."

We drove for a few hours, and I couldn't take my eyes off him. He smiled to me; it made me happy. We both were lucky to have each other.

Then we reached our destination. It was the high cliff over the sea that we visited before. Right behind the cliff there was a giant horizon over the sea. The place looked as wonderful as the first time I saw it.

You could sit right on the cliff and look into the endless sea. The view was mesmerizing. I pressed harder into Peter's chest. We stayed close to each other looking at the view. It looked like something from a picture.

"Thank you for bringing me here."

"I'm happy you like it."

"Sure, it's your special place."

"Yes, you are right."

That minute I knew that I was really important to him. We both were happy, both in love and the world was in sync. It was wonderful. I loved that man, and he was my one true love. It was one of the most important moments in my life. I knew he would never leave me. This place was special to him, and he choses to share it with me. I was excited; I knew that today I opened a new chapter in my life, a chapter full of love and confidence. We got ourselves near one of the trees. He had his arms around me. I pressed closer to his chest. It was one of those moments that made my heart sing. I wanted this moment to last forever. He suddenly kissed me. I felt warmth all over my body. His kisses were wonderful, and he truly was into me. I liked his every touch; we honestly had the chemistry going. I knew that he was happy with me, and it made me feel safe. He made me feel loved and desired. Peter, his emotions and that view from a cliff—it was really something from a fairytale; I could never have imagined it even if I tried. I was happy beyond my wildest dreams. After some time, we both returned to the gravicar and he drove me home.

"See you later, Evelyn. I had a magnificent time."

"I had a splendid time too. Could we do this again?"

"Of course. I will be thinking about you."

"I will also. See you later."

"See you."

When I got inside my house, my feelings were a mess. I was thinking about a hundred things in a minute. Nobody teaches you at school about that, you just have to experience it. Love is mad. It's like a fire burning inside and brightening our way in life. It's a miracle that nobody believes is possible, but when you find the one true love in your life, that's more than winning a billion dollars in a lottery. If you don't believe me, wait until you experience it. It's like a Christmas present that you were waiting for all your life and when you finally find it, it means more than every gift you ever got. What is more important, it's no dream. This is reality. I lay in my bed just to stay calm for a while, my mind was in chaos, so many thoughts, and it's really hard to control them all. But one thing stands out from others; I really wanted to be with Peter all my life. He was the most important person in my life. Then I got a call from Max.

"Hello, sis."

"Hello, brother."

"You seem different."

"What do you mean?"

"Something is really different about you."

"What do you mean?"

"You're blushing."

"I'm not."

Then I saw the doctor standing next to Max.

"Hello," I said to her.

"Hello, Evelyn."

"How is my brother treating you?"

"He's pretty nice. He's a very good person."

"That's good to hear. Do you like him?"

"He's pretty wonderful."

"Thank you for the compliments," my brother said, looking a bit embarrassed.

"Don't mention it, you're a great guy," she said.

"You know, sis. I got a promotion. I'm a lieutenant now."

"That's great. I knew you would make it."

"Thanks."

"See you, Max, and see you, too, Angela.

"So long, Evelyn," said Angela.

"See you, sis."

I was happy for my brother; he was really worth the promotion. I wanted to do something useful too. I wanted to help my parents more. I went out into the fields and helped plant the potatoes. The work was hard, but I enjoyed it. There was a lot of work to be done, so I invited Peter, he helped around a little. I felt closer to him. I saw something good in his eyes when we were in the fields, he tried his best and that was all that mattered. He lent his helping hand to our family. It felt like he was doing it all the time, he even taught some things to me and to my parents—not only was he an excellent engineer, but he was a good farmer too. I saw the determination in his eyes, and I liked a man who wasn't afraid to get his hands dirty. He was really charming working in those fields planting potatoes. It was a great outdoor activity. It seemed like a wonderful and well spent time. Hopefully, we will have many more days like this. I was happy to help my parents, and glad to be close to someone as Peter.

When we all were finished, Mom decided that we all should go to church tomorrow. I thought it was a good idea, and I just wanted to spend some time at the church. People in the church were nice and made up a community. You could feel closer to more people and feel the unity that surrounded us all. Mom said that there is some sort of good atmosphere within the church, people who pray sometimes got their prayers answered, and that was the most magical thing about the world. I wanted to bring Peter, too. He seemed a bit lost lately, and I wanted to spend more time with him.

"Peter do you want to go to church with me?"

"Yes I would like that."

"OK then we will meet tomorrow, see you later."

The morning was bright. All that morning sun quickly brightened up my day. I was full of happiness because everything was fine, everything was going great. To be so close to nature was a warm feeling. My mom called for me later.

"It's time for church," she said.

"Mom, wait for me a little."

I fell into the fields, and my heart was bursting. I loved nature, and being a part of it was the most magnificent feeling of them all. Then I saw Peter. He was coming to pick up my mom and me.

"Hello, Peter."

"Hello there, beautiful."

I hugged him and kissed him softly on his lips. He pressed closer to me, and so we stood there for some time, looking in each other's eyes, like we just met for the first time, it was amazing, we both felt joy and happiness and all we needed was to look into each other and feel those warm emotions of happiness that filled our hearts. At this moment, we had each other, and the world didn't matter. Nothing mattered. We were in love, and we understood each other without worlds. That moment was perfect; I couldn't imagine it, even if I wanted to.

"Come on kids let's go."

We both sat down inside and were holding hands and looking at each other smiling.

"So how are you there, you lovebirds?

"We are fine mom, thanks. We are just happy," I answered.

"Oh, that young love. I know I remember your father. He was really handsome and charming; I loved him because he always could see the bright side of life. I had a bad day and was walking all sad and deeply concerned for my future, and then your father asked me out all of a sudden. He only wanted to keep my spirits up. He talked about his adventures in childhood and his memories of school; he told all these stories with a portion of humor and just brightened up my day. We met a few times more and then another time, and we slowly fell in love, he was the man I couldn't live without; he was that bright spark in my life. And I knew that this would be the man I would spend my life together."

"That's a wonderful story," I said.

"It's fate and you can't run from it, when it's true love, it just is. I see both of you. You seem happy, but there is a long way ahead. Life isn't easy, and real love must be cherished. Love is like a small flower, if you don't take care of it, the leaves will fall, and it will fade away."

"What did you like about dad the most?"

"Everything. I liked everything about him. Your dad is the most wonderful person I have ever met. His heart is pure. His mind is sharp, and he simply is charming, not selfish, imaginative and most important in love with me."

Finally, we arrived at the church. That was a small, but a cozy place, and it was full of people. There was a wedding happening. The couple looked really beautiful, the family members of the groom and the bride gathered to participate in this event. The woman had a wonderful long white dress, and the groom had a tight black suit. I could tell from their eyes that they were happy; they looked at each other with so much love and with such smiles that could melt even the coldest of hearts. Peter took my hand, looked at me, and we both felt joy for the newlyweds. We said our prayers and wished them all the best. After all, only the ones who truly love can understand others in such a moment of joy. When newlyweds got their blessings, they went out of the church holding hands with each other.

"I hope we will be happy together like them," I said.

"I hope that too," Responded Peter.

Peter kissed me and later we looked at each other and smiled. We were happy for us, for our parents, for that couple. We were in the clouds. Life was getting better and better. We all returned home.

"How was the church?

"Great, we saw a wedding.

"Oh, that's wonderful. I remember me and your mother. We were so much in love that we even got late into our own wedding? Do you remember my love?"

"Yes, I remember," she said. "It was all because of that bachelor's party. Until this day, I don't know what you did on that day, but I trust you anyway."

"Honey it was harmless. I just forgot my suit at the cleaners. It's a really fun story."

She smiled. "OK, you can tell us later. The most important thing is that we have a wonderful family."

"Yes, honey, we sure do."

My dad kissed my mom. I felt that they were really into each other. Even after so many years, they were still so much in love. My parents' love made me feel great and gave me comfort. They looked happy, and that's all that mattered. Everything was fine. I was feeling wonderful. Peter was beside me; he looked into my eyes and smiled. He saw right through me. He was a wonderful person; I loved him for this deep look and many other things. I could say he had a spark, something that was really attractive. I didn't know what it was, but I felt it all the time I was with him. He was the man of my life. I just loved him.

Then it was all over the news. It had begun. The AI started massive attacks on the human colonies. The machines had very powerful spaceships. We had lots of battleships too, but the machines had more advanced ships. Most of them cut through our defenses. The casualties were high on both sides, but they just kept coming in. How could they build an army so fast? It was unthinkable. We managed to build our fleet over many years, but they must be using some sort of new technology. On holoTV, I saw how they boarded a ship. When they cut through steel, they used animal-like machines to fight our troops, machines like tigers, lions, and wolfs were all over the place. It was horrible. The animal-like robots had knife-sharp skin that cut through almost anything. I left the room and puked. I would never forget what I saw that day. It was one of the most horrible things I had ever seen. I wanted to forget everything and went outside. Peter followed me outside and hugged me. I felt a warm breeze of air. I had no more strength to see that horrible view no more, and I just wanted a breath of fresh air. Nature looked wonderful. It was different. I appreciated it more and more. Nothing was more wonderful than life, why do machines want to destroy everything? Can we live in peace? Or are they mad, driven by the idea of ending our civilization? If the machines don't appreciate life, what will they do next? Do they want to take their own place in the universe, or do they want to take ours? I sat in the field of rye, that magnificent and peaceful field. I felt calm when I had nature and life around me, it was wonderful to be one with nature. It helped me to relax. Peter was with me all the time and supported me the best he could. I remembered something from school. Professor Hawking said: "Where there is life, there is hope." I still believed we had hope. Even in the hardest moments of life, there was some sense that everything would be fine no matter what. That hope makes us fall in love, it makes us do our best, and it makes us fight in spite of when the odds are not in our favor. Peter had to leave. He had some work at home, we said our goodbyes, and I went home. I called Max.

"How are you brother?

"Thank you, sis, I'm doing pretty fine. We will be attacking the enemy soon. The preparations have been made for the big fight against the enemy."

"You have to do your best. They are not human. They are machines. They have no feelings."

"However, we have a big surprise for them."

"What is it?"

"It's classified. Don't think about it, sis. Everything will be fine. We will take care of them."

"I hope you do because if not, they will come after all of us."

"We stopped them the first time; we won't slow down this time either.

"I hope we stop them."

"I hope so too, sis. I really hope so."

I was glad to hear that they might have some weapon against the machines. After all, we were facing a great danger if we failed, they would stop for nobody—not for women, for old people or even for children. If we didn't do something soon, we might face extinction. We needed to do something; we needed to face the enemy.

On that significant day, I invited Peter and his mother over to our house. I just wanted to be closer to the people that were important to me. Anne, Josh, Annabel, James, and Robert were with their parents in their homes. It was all over the news, our biggest fleet assembled at one location and wanted to strike the enemy as hard as they could and with everything they had. It was a big stand against the machines; every man knew what he was doing. Soldiers knew that they were fighting for existence. Not for resources, not for glory or power, but for the people they loved: their mothers, their wives, their children, their grandparents, and all of humankind. Nothing was more important than this. The stakes were high. Every crew member on the spaceships, every pilot in the fighters, every trooper in the launch pads, and everyone at home watching the screens of their holoTVs knew that this moment would determine the outcome of this war. There was a huge gathering of the spaceships; all the human fleet was assembled. The enemy was nearing our positions.

Then it began. The enemies were spotted on the radars. The fleet opened fire. The machines were swarming. There were so many of them. Lots and lots kept coming in, the fleet held on as long as they could. It was a spectacular view. You could see giant human spaceships with huge plasma canons opening fire on everything they saw. Carriers launched all of their fighters. Cruisers' and corvettes' laser fire was seen all over the place. I saw lasers of all possible colors, and that was a battle no one had ever seen before. Heavy canons were blasting everything in sight. Fighters were scattered all over the place. It was a massive battleground.

I knew my brother wouldn't stay in one place; he was probably in a fighter blowing away AI drones from the open space. I knew he was really angry at the machines and the only way to show that anger was blowing up as many enemy ships as possible. I knew he was a great pilot, so probably now the machines are having a hard time dealing with him.

Finally, when the enemy was all over our positions, the human fleet used their secret weapon. On the dreadnought "Independence," they had a huge EMP weapon; our superiors fired an enormous burst of EMP energy. We could see the EMP energy wave spreading through the open space. The machines became inoperable. They just stood still. The weapon stopped them. It probably fried their circuits, and we could see people cheering all over the place. People were happy, hugging each other, cheering, jumping from one place to the other. Humanity was happy to finally defeat such a huge enemy. There were so many smiles, like I have never seen before.

However, after a few minutes, my dad shouted: "Look!" The machines one by one were becoming operational again. The battle continued.

We stood our ground as best as we could, but one by one our battleships and the whole fleet was demolished. Only our best ship was left standing. "Independence" was our last hope. This ship stood firm as long as it could, and then we saw her perform a hyperspace jump. It was all over. Our last hope was gone.

When I got outside, I saw it. "Independence" jumped to Earth. I could see her floating over one of our cities. I called my brother.

"Max, how are you?

"We failed, Evelyn. We failed badly."

"How are you? How is Angela?"

"She is fine, but she has lots of work now."

"How is the captain?"

"I am the captain now."

"What do you mean?"

"I'm the high-ranking officer on the ship. Every officer is dead."

"How did it happen?"

"When the machines regained their strength, we opened fire on everything. However, they cut through the steel and went for our main hyperspace cores. We exterminated them, but with a heavy crew loss. Two of our three hyperspace cores were damaged and leaking. Our captain ran to the machinery section to manually initiate the last core and bring us to safety. It was his act of bravery that saved us. Somehow he chose this planet for his last jump. He had a huge dose of antimatter radiation. He could never have survived. He is a hero. We will bury him with honor, he saved us all. We owe everything to him. What's more, we captured one of the AI majors. He was struggling very hard, but we manage to contain him behind a force field."

"So he's like a human?"

"At least, he pretended he was. He's much stronger, and he led the attack on our ship."

"What's next?"

"We will gather our strength and strike one last time."

"And you will lose."

"We have no other choice.

"You do. Have you made any progress decoding that ancient energy crystal?"

"We tried everything, but we still have nothing."

"Try harder, its humanity's last hope."

"I will do my best, but if we fail, we will have our last dance with the enemy."

I knew that everything was bad. We lost so many people, and the machines now were on the killing spree. I felt devastated. I never knew that this would be so bad. I was scared for those people because I didn't know what would happen, the machines, they were only machines; they had no value for human life. The war was coming to us, and I was scared like never before, what those monsters would do to our people, what they would do to our families, we just wanted peace and that's all.

It was scary. I ran back to Peter crying. He was upset and angry; he only wanted to destroy the machines.

"Peter, I'm scared."

He hugged me; I saw the love in his eyes and his wonderful smile.

"I love you. I won't let anything happen to you."

"I love you too."

"Yes, but I'd rather die standing. I will protect you."

"I know."

"Everything I need, I have on this planet. Do you love me?"

"Yes, I do."

Then Peter bent on one knee and smiled at me. I could see his blue eyes sparkling, his smile shining bright as day. He reached inside his pocket and presented me a beautiful ring. It was small but elegant, it was slightly curved with a small Blue Diamond. I knew Peter didn't have much, but I also knew he invested all of his money into that ring. It was such a beautiful moment; I started shivering and nearly cried. Then looking into my eyes, he whispered: "Do you want to marry me?"

"Yes, of course, I love you."

I cried from excitement and hugged him as hard as I could. Then he put the ring on my finger. It was a precious moment.

"I know a small church where we could be married. It would be fine for me," Peter said to me.

"Yes, I think so too. I don't want something big, just something for you, me, and the family."

"Yes I agree."

"When will we marry?" I asked.

"I made a few arrangements. We will marry soon."

Our parents knew everything. They came up closer to us. Mom and dad hugged us both. They looked pleased. Despite everything that was going on, I was joyful. At least, I had some hope for the future, and that was all I needed.

"Remember that small church we visited?" he asked.

"Yes I remember."

"The priest agreed to marry us."

"That's great."

"I'm glad you're happy."

"Of course, I am. You know I love you."

"I love you too."

We all went back into the living room. Dad opened a bottle of champagne. I felt good. I had hope, even in those times I felt a glimpse of light. Somehow, I knew in my heart that everything will be fine. Maybe seeing all my loved ones happy made me forget all about the war, the horror, and the despair that we all felt after that battle with the most powerful enemy we as a species had ever faced.

After a few days, Anne came into my place to help me prepare. I had no dress. I had no makeup. I was stressed like never before. Today would still be the happiest day of my life. I felt happy, but sad at the same time, there were so many emotions in my head. I felt like I was going to burst from all the thoughts in my mind. I knew Peter was exceptional; in fact, we both were special to each other. I also knew I loved him more than any other man in my life.

Everything in this life has a meaning. I was getting married to the man I loved the most, but there was a storm coming in our direction. I didn't know what to do, how to stop it. I wanted to be glad, just to be happy, but those horrible things, those machines. I wanted to cry. Everything was going great. It was going just perfect, but why now, why had humanity made this horrible mistake, why had our greed and our blind will to play God brought us to this. I'm just a simple girl. I wanted to marry, to have kids, but I'm not certain of the future. Truthfully I'm scared. Anne came to the room.

"Hello there, fortunate one," she said.

"Yes I'm lucky, but a little distracted."

"Every bride is distracted," she acknowledge. "That is nothing new. Just be you and everything will be fine."

"Excellent. I knew you have a good sense of humor, Anne. But after a few weeks, there will be no you, no me, no Peter, no mom, no dad, and no school; AIs will wipe out everything. We will be just memories long forgotten in the sands of this planet."

Ann looked at me seriously. "Now you listen to me very carefully, because I will say it only once. You have a wonderful person waiting for you; you have a great family, who want to see you happy, maybe for the last time in your life. So what if the end of humanity as we know it is coming. You have to remember one thing. This moment, this place, those people who love you and this world on this day are yours, don't let any tin can or piece of metal ruin that. Because if you give up now, that means they have already won. That means that those evil, metallic, soulless creatures that are raging all over our worlds are victorious. You are not doing it for yourself. You're doing it for everybody in this village. You're doing it because you have a strong spirit and a heart of gold, nobody else is like you, Evelyn. I've met lots of people throughout my life, but you, you are an inspiration to me. Do you think I'm wrong? I hope not. So quit whining, get dressed and be happy."

"Thanks, Anne. I think I know what you mean. But where will I get a dress, makeup and everything else?"

"I knew you would ask that. You remind me of my mom. She was a wonderful person. That's why we got along so well. I took her wedding dress, and I bet you will fit in it just perfect. I will leave you now. Try it on."

I'd never seen anything more beautiful than that dress. It was simple and elegant. It was a mini wedding dress, and it ended above the knees. At first, it seemed like a simple cocktail dress. It had gorgeous mini length, perfectly balanced by the long fitted sleeves and open neckline. It was made from cotton lace, and it was impeccably crafted. It had a full skirt, which is as easy to wear, as it is strikingly beautiful. Fitted through the bodice and nipped at the waist, it accentuated the figure. The dress was fully lined except for the sleeves. The sleeves had handcrafted elements, which looked like white flowers that were covering the whole hands. It looked magnificent. I never had seen anything like it. It was really beautiful.

When Anne saw me in the dress, she just smiled and hugged me.

"You look wonderful in that dress," she exclaimed.

"Thank you, Anne."

"Now let's add some makeup."

After a friendly chat and playing a few hours with the makeup box, Ann thought I was ready."

"Just look in the mirror," she said, "you are shining."

When I looked at the mirror for the first time, I couldn't recognize myself. I had never seen myself look so beautiful before. My eyes looked really big, because of the darker shades and my lips looked full and handsome like cherries.

"Now for the final touch."

She brought out a pair of pearl earrings.

"Where did you get those?" I asked, amazed by their beauty.

"Those were my moms. I will lend them to you."

They made me look gorgeous.

After I was dressed, my dad came in.

"I am ready. I'm so happy, Dad."

"I know you are darling. I can see it in your eyes."

We all sat down in the gravicar. I was excited and a little nervous. I knew that this day would change everything, and I just wanted to be happy. I looked through the window and in those fields of grain; I could see my young days passing by. It was a new beginning for me. I was just pleased to be here, to remember my past and to have hope for the future. When the gravicar stopped, I stepped out and saw the church. It was beautiful. My dad took my hand. He was happy to give me away. We took our first steps to the altar. The whole village was here. All the people from the town gathered to see Peter and me getting married. It was the first time ever that I saw so many people. All of them wanted to see hope. They all wanted to feel that happiness that surrounded us. Father took me near the altar; I kissed him and stood beside Peter. I had never seen such beauty; the altar was covered in flowers of all colors, sorts, and sizes. I couldn't remember them all, even if I wanted to. And that excellent aroma, I felt that flavor the first morning in our new home on Earth. I remember it because it was the most wonderful smell I ever experienced. Peter took my hand. I was shaking a little. I felt nervous. I never had experienced this feeling. It felt like I had shivers all over my body.

The priest began the ceremony. "We have gathered here for this lovely couple to love and to hold each other for the rest of their days."

Everyone in the church stayed still. Some women started to cry.

"Peter, do you take Evelyn to be your wife? Do you promise to be true to her in good times and in bad, in sickness and in health, to love her and honor her all the days of your life?"

"I do."

"Evelyn, do you take Peter to be your husband? Do you promise to be true to him in good times and in bad, in sickness and in health, to love him and honor him all the days of your life?

"I do."

"What God has joined, men must not divide. Now please the rings."

Robert gave Peter the ring. Peter gently put it on my finger. Anne gave me Peter's ring, and I put it on his.

"I now pronounce you man & wife. You may kiss the bride."

Peter sunk into my lips, and we were almost in the clouds. I never felt so much love flowing through me. I had never experienced so much happiness before. I was like a child who got the most perfect present I could ever have. There was a wonderful feeling of freedom and happiness in my heart. My life was going the right way, and I was the happiest person in the world. We looked in each other's eyes. It was like looking in the mirror. He was a part of me, and I was a part of him, and I knew he would do anything for me. He would love me and treat me the way a man should treat a woman, and he would do anything to protect me, even at the cost of his life.

Peter took my hand, and we both took our first steps as husband and wife. I saw all the people in our small village gathered in the church. They looked at us like at some new hope for the new world that is bashing all the doors and is coming our way. I knew that the danger was close, but somehow today everything faded away. It seemed like those machines, and the war was far away.

After the ceremony, we drove away in the gravicar somewhere that we could spend some time alone with each other. Peter drove to the place that was important to both of us. It was that window to the sea. We sat on the edge of a cliff. The whole sea opened for us. The sun was sitting down. I felt I could sit here until the end of times.

"How do you feel?" Peter asked me.

"I am excited. Today was a wonderful day. I love you," I told him joyfully.

"I love you too."

"Do you believe we might have a future?" I asked.

"I think we have today and that is all that matters.

"I think so too."

I kissed him on the lips; then he sank into my lips and slowly went around my neck. I shivered. His kisses were slow. It felt like we were kissing for the first time. He was gentle and sweet. He slowly went to my shoulder and kissed me there. I looked into his eyes and smiled. His beautiful blue eyes looked at me. I could see the ocean on one side and his deep-blue eyes on the other. I couldn't decide which was more beautiful—the ocean or his eyes. The sun was setting down. We looked at each other smiling, and it felt like we just met for the first time. He took my hand, and we walked to the gravicar. We drove to a little hotel near the seashore. It was very small, but it had windows to the sea. We rented a room. I was very nervous, but he hugged me and smiled.

We went into the room. The view from the window was magnificent. I could see the sun setting down, and it felt like the sun was being eaten by the sea. The sea was calm; I almost didn't see any waves. In the room, there was a bed white as snow. I sat on the bed and Peter sat next to me.

"Do you like it here?" he asked.

"Every place with you in it is wonderful."

He leaned his head and slowly kissed me on the lips. Then he went around my neck. The kisses were soft and gentle. He wasn't rushing. We were just enjoying the moment. He went lower and reached my shoulder. I shivered and smiled. He looked at me, put his hand on my head and sucked into my lips. Then he slowly took off my wedding dress, and we both were lying on the bed. I felt his warm body close to me. I can only tell you that night was the most memorable and wonderful night I ever had and every small detail is only between me and Peter.

I woke up early. His strong body was beside me. He woke up, kissed me on the lips and started tickling me. I giggled. Then he went into the kitchen to get me some tea. We sat down, looking into the sea and just relaxed. I pressed closer to him. The view through the window was really beautiful.

"What now?

"We fix the 'Independence' and get back at those dammed AIs."

I stood still and understood that these days would be some of the last days we would speak with each other, and soon he would be attacking the drones and enemy spaceships. I wished this wouldn't end that way, and I could do something.

"I would like to spend all of my days with you, but I have to go soon."

"Yes, I know. We could spend our last time just like that: looking in the sky, looking in each other's eyes."

"You are a wonder you know."

"You are wonderful too."

We stood there for some time, and I looked into Peter's eyes. They felt sad. I tried to cheer him up, but he was somewhere else. I took him home; he was full of anger and despair.

There were my brother, father, Robert, Josh, Annabel, James, and Anne. They all seemed concerned. The news wasn't good, and the universe seemed dark for all of us. There were a lot of sad faces, almost everybody was without hope. The table seemed grey and colorless, only sadness was felt in the room.

"That dammed Everton. It's his fault," I said.

"Yes. Somebody wanted to play God, and we have what we have," said Max.

"I would like to see him in the eyes," I thought aloud.

"You could do that tomorrow. I'll be back on the ship, fixing the drives, weapons, gathering some new crewmen. You could see him then. However, I doubt he is worth it."

"I want to see him; I want to know what was on his mind when he started all of this."

Next day, I went to the ship. There was a little place for Everton. He was in a small baggage room. He was sleeping on the floor next to the crates that were lying all around. He was all alone, locked in an empty room. He was hated by everyone. Nobody cared about his life. He was so empty and so lost.

"I never knew I would see a monster in my life!" I exclaimed when I saw him.

"I know you hate me, but I never knew it would end this way," Everton argued.

"You should have given it a thought or two before you did it!"

Everton lowered his head. He looked sad and lost. I felt sorry for him.

"We are the victims of our own creations," Everton suddenly said.

"Yes and how you are going to stop this. You made it real. You should stop it."

I punched his chest with my fists as hard as I could and started to cry.

"It's already out of my control," he said.

"But you must have a kill switch or something?"

"That EMP field *was* the kill switch; it didn't work."

"There has to be a solution."

Everton nodded his head. "Most of the time there is one. You just have to see the details."

"What details?" I asked.

"The little things, the answers are always in the small things, small details that we miss."

"You are crazy."

I was angry and left him there. I wanted to scream, to shout, but that was the moment of my weakness. However, it wasn't my individual weakness. This technology that dates back to World War II, the technology we created to improve our communication, our free time, our social behaviors, the power of high-tech growing economies we used for entertainment, for our good or evil purposes was now rampaging through our worlds and only our own madness, and our personal decisions had led us to this place. We were addicted. This wasn't a simple addiction; it's not alcohol, not drugs, not sex. It's a drug of technology. We had the illusion of control, the illusion of escape, the illusion of wealth, the wrong ideals and false values. We thought we could control something like this, but there was no control. We hoped a false hope, but we didn't understand that the only salvation was in ourselves and on our dependence on others not on the machines.

However, we were fighting bravely. Everything in our minds and our souls was fighting the menace. Our forces gathered from all parts of the universe: for every sector, every planet, every piece of the land, every house, every meter, the machines were having massive losses. The metal of the machines was met with heavy resistance, because the people's hearts were stronger than any metal could ever be. We stood our ground as hard as we could. Lasers were piercing metal robots all the way. Every man and woman fought as hard as they could to slow the machines down. We were strong and united like never before and no AI could take that away from us. We were fighting our best fight, and the harder the machines pressed us, the harder we fought back. The enemy faced heavy losses, and the spirit of our people grew stronger with every small victory. Our veins filled with human blood were resisting the machines every step of the way.

I cried for all those people that were in such terrible circumstances because I knew that human life is precious and machines, they didn't stop, not for anything. They destroyed planets and ecosystems. They didn't value life, and that was the scariest and most horrible thing that flashed in their synthetic brains. I understood this. Machines were the enemy of all life. They didn't stop for trees. They didn't stop for flowers, not for animals, not for insects. They had no value for life. That was their fatal flaw.

Somehow I felt sick and puked into the toilet. Then I understood it. I was pregnant. I was happy in this moment, but I didn't want to tell anyone, especially not Peter. Not now. I promised myself to do everything in my power to raise this child and to stop those soulless machines.

I didn't know what I had to do, I was so lost and so desperate. I knew I would lose Peter soon. I couldn't accept that. I was so lost. I needed time for myself. So I visited the church that Peter and I got married in. I bent on my knees and prayed. I prayed for all the people who were fighting the machines, for the people who died fighting the enemy, all the children who lost their parents and all the parents who lost their children. Then the priest came up to me.

"Are you alright?" the priest asked me.

"No, I'm desperate."

"You have to be strong. I know it's hard in these times, but you must be strong."

"Why this is happening to us," I asked.

"We choose it by ourselves. It's our own choice, now we must face the consequences."

"There must be something."

"God is the way."

"What do you mean?"

"God is light that shows us our destination in life, so we must trust in him."

In that moment, I understood everything. Everything was clear, like something opened my mind. I understood what I must do.

At this moment, I was in the clouds.

"Thank you, you really helped me."

"God be with you child."

I called Peter as fast as I could.

"Pick me up! Pick me up now!!!"

"What is wrong?"

"Just pick me up, please!"

After a few minutes, Peter was there with a gravicar. He asked me what's wrong, but I just asked him to get me to the "Independence." I was so fond of the idea. I didn't feel myself at all. My brother was on the ground with some crew loading some modules to the "Independence."

"Max, can you give me the crystal?"

"Why? We checked it. It's no use."

"Just give me a try."

"Why? We checked it with everything we could. Multiple lasers, artificial sunlight from different solar systems, everything we had.

"Please trust me. Not everything."

"Ok. Just because you're my sister, I will give you a try. Nevertheless, it seems stupid."

He gave me a crystal. I had never seen anything more beautiful. I ran next to the nearest tree and put the crystal between the shade and the Earth's sun, so that the light from the sun reflected in the shade of a tree.

"It's no use. We tried everything.

And then it happened. We could see a galactic map reflecting from the crystal. It was amazing, so much detail and so precise.

"I don't believe my eyes."

"Do you trust me now?"

"But we checked everything. We used artificial sunlight from Earth too."

"However, not the real sunlight."

"No. Not the real one."

The scientist quickly adapted their scanners and found a secret location on the reflected map.

"We have hope," I said.

"I truly hope you are right. I really hope so."

My brother quickly ordered his people to be faster with the repairs and prepare the ship.

"I want to go," I said.

"I want to go too," added Peter.

"Ok. Peter you will go with me. However, you have to stay on Earth, Evelyn."

"No I won't.

"Please, it's too dangerous.

"You will need me.

"Be reasonable.

"I found that map for a reason. I will do something important. I feel it."

"OK. I will take you on the ship, but you have to listen to me, be careful, and don't interfere."

"OK. I will."

The crew gathered weapons, the entire tech and all the supplies it could, there were a few repairs left to be made to the "Independence," but after that the ship was ready for the journey. The scientists calculated the path to the destination. It was really far and we needed a few more jumps than expected, so the repair crew and some volunteers from Earth put all their efforts into fixing another hyperspace core, so the ship would have two cores running. Max didn't like my presence on the ship, but he had no other choice, after all I was the one who discovered the secret of the crystal.

Everyone was anxious. We had a big journey ahead. Hopefully, we will come back with an ally against the machines. Of course if we return at all. My brother had his new captain uniform on. He looked sharp and confident. It seemed he was a different person; I had to look up to him now. The coordinates were set. We jumped.

The first jump was completed safely. The cores had to recharge, so the "Independence" sent out a lookout mission. There were lots of asteroids and a few gas-giant planets, they looked really big, and there was also a star nearby with a few planets, one of which had four moons.

"Commander we picked up large debris," said an officer.

"What kind? The machines couldn't be here; this sector had to be empty. We are too far away from the conflict zone."

"Sir I don't pick up AI signatures, there're only lots of our signatures and some of them more than 300 years old."

"Run the database, we are missing something."

"Right away sir."

Then there was the signal on the main channel.

"Hello, little friends."

"Who are you? Identify your selves."

"We are your friendly welcoming party."

"Please identify?"

"We like your ship. It looks like it has lots of value."

"We are on a mission. You are ordered to stand down."

"Ha ha ha, the young boy wants us to stand down. Let's give them a welcoming party, boys!"

There were signals of incoming ships all over the place, from small to medium-sized vessels; they were attacking with everything they had.

"I have some info, sir. This appears to have been a warzone 100 years ago, and those people and ships are what are left of the survivors. Apparently now, this is a big pirate zone."

"Engineering, how are our hyperspace cores?" asked the captain, my brother.

"We can't jump. We need more time," an engineer reported back.

"How much?"

"30 minutes," replied the engineer.

"I give you five."

"But—"

"Just do it!

The pirates were all over us; they used their heavy weapons and wanted to target our engines. Max ordered pilots to protect the engines. That was the most important part of a ship, and he protected it with everything he had. This was the most important part of a ship and if the engines went off, we all would be stuck in this place, and our ship would be stripped down for parts. Max ordered the ship to use everything it had against the enemies. Pirates attached trooper pods to get inside the hull of the ship. A few levels were breached, but soldiers were giving pirates a tough fight and the people of the "Independence" were holding.

A call came up from engineering "We are ready to jump."

"Do it."

The second jump was a success. We were in some unknown sector. There was lots of empty space and lots of disturbance on the radar; you could only see the clouds of dust, yellow, green, and red. I had never seen such a view. This place looked like a picture from a fairytale.

Then suddenly we received the first contact. It was a ship of an unknown configuration. The radar couldn't get a lock on in. It seemed the ship was reflecting and jamming the signal. Then I heard it for the first time. I was shocked a little, but I understood that those creatures communicate telepathically.

Who are you?

"We are humans from Earth."

My brother and Peter thought I was talking to myself.

What is your mission?

"We seek help."

What kind of help do you seek?

"Our race is in danger."

Then the alien ship disabled all our weapon systems and gave us coordinates.

"What now?" asked Peter.

"We follow. We have no other choice," answered Max.

We jumped using the coordinates from the ship. The first time I saw it, I couldn't believe my eyes. Their planet was fully covered with crystals. It seemed that the planet was a big round crystal, the structures were enormous.

We are expecting you.

Me, Max, and Peter took a shuttle and landed on the planet's surface. We were greeted by an alien that looked similar to a bee in our planet. The creature had four spiky legs on its abdomen and stood strait with its chest held high like a human. On the back of its chest, it had something similar to the wings of a bee. The head didn't resemble a bee's head at all. It was more similar to a mantis, but longer and with deep black eyes. In fact, the alien looked like a hybrid of a bee and a mantis.

I wondered in my head, did it have a stinger?

Somehow the creature answered the question in my head telepathically.

Yes, I have a stinger, but I use it only when necessary.

We started to communicate. Peter and my brother didn't know what was happening, they didn't hear the alien speaking. So I calmed them down and said that everything was fine.

Why are you here?

"We seek help."

Why?

"We needed hope."

Hope?

"It's the last chance for anything.

Why do you need a last chance?

"We are fighting an enemy that is stronger than us.

The alien looked me with his eyes, and I felt like he was in my mind looking for something, searching.

You created this enemy by yourselves. It's your child; you have to take care of your own problems.

The alien wanted to send me away, but I begged him not to.

"Please. It's out of control. I beg, please just listen to us."

The alien looked at me; he looked into my belly, stood still for a moment and told in my mind.

These two must stay here. You will follow me.

"Peter, Max. You must stay."

"But why?"

"You must trust me, just stay here."

The alien took me on a crystal shuttle. We were flying somewhere. It was a city of crystals. Everywhere and everything was made of them—roads, buildings, transportation. Everything was bright and shining in the beautiful crystal light. The city was full of life. Everything was moving. Some of the aliens used their wings to fly, but most of them used the crystal transportation. The place was like one big crystal. It looked like those crystals are grown, they could be strong, they could be light, and they made everything from them. These crystals were the basis of their civilization. I felt that the alien didn't like what I understood, but he didn't show it. He didn't care a lot, because they were so ahead of us that in a million years, we couldn't reach their level. Not only that, but the crystal technology made them strong. They seemed very organized. They worked like a single organism.

We were heading to a large crystal, the biggest I had ever seen; it resembled a big citadel or a castle. We were greeted by an alien who looked much bigger and stronger than the first one. He took me inside the crystal palace. It was magnificent. It was enormous and full of giant crystals from wonderful colors. It seemed like a dream, and some crystals even moved making crystal sculptures of aliens, and another crystal forms that I couldn't understand. Then I saw two big guards and the gate. Those guards were really colossal, twice as bigger than the ones who greeted me. They looked scary, and they looked into my guide and quickly opened the door. There was a huge hall and at the end of that hall was a giant throne. That was the first time I saw her. She was huge, five times bigger than the other aliens I had encountered. Then I understood that she was the Queen. Next to her throne, there were 10 of her councilors—five at one side and five at the other. She communicated telepathically with me.

Come closer child, don't be afraid.

I was scared and I knew she felt that, she looked very powerful, strong, and wise. The other aliens around her, seemed truly scary too.

I will not eat you. I promise.

Slowly, I came closer to the throne.

"I came to...

I know why you have come here.

"You do? How?

I know all the thoughts of my subjects, so I let you inside.

"Then you will help us."

Why should I help you?

"Please our people are dying.

I'm not interested in your people. I just wanted to meet the last of your species. Everybody dies; it's a way of life. You created something you can't control; now you will pay the price.

"Nevertheless, why did you ask me here?

You're a mother like me, and this is your first child. I wanted to feel the love of a firstborn to remember that feeling. Can I look inside your mind?

"Yes, you can, only if you look at the enemy we are facing.

You are giving me orders!!! No one since the Great War with my sisters has given me orders!!!

Everyone in the room stood still, like they had seen lightning hit a tree in front of them.

"I'm not giving any orders. I'm only asking for you to look inside my mind, and you will understand yourself that this enemy is even more dangerous than the one you have battled before."

OK, my child, but this will not be pleasant. You asked for it yourself. I will tap into your deepest memories, see your darkest secrets, and if I don't like something that I see I might even kill you. Are you prepared for that?

"I have no other choice."

Just open your mind, think of your thoughts like water, it flows softly and slowly. Just let your thoughts flow, relax and don't think about anything. It will hurt a little, but I see no other choice.

I tried to be calm. I remembered the open fields. I remembered those wonderful empty fields. I was so happy there. Slowly, I felt her going through my mind. It was easy at first, and she tried to be gentle as possible. I remembered my friends on Ella, my childhood, my school. I remembered all the good things and fun things. Like the kiss of my mother when she got me to sleep, the fairytales of my father, when he came back from work, my grandmother that took care of me, my older brother when we used to play with him when we were kids, then I remembered how my parents used to argue, then my head hurt a little. I remembered how we left Ella, how we found a brand new home. I remembered the open fields, the wonderful nature, the new friends, then I remembered the riots on Ella through holoTV, my head hurt a little more, but I relaxed and felt better. I remembered Peter, our first kiss, my happy family, my brother's accomplishments, then I remembered the first miner ship encounter with enemy AI, the first time it destroyed a star base, my head started to feel bad. I remembered that I was with Peter and my family all the time, watching how the beasts of steel destroyed the whole planet and everything that was living on it, my head was in real pain, but I knew that I had to go on, I knew that the Queen must see everything, she must know, so I tried to be calm. I remembered how the machines became stronger and more powerful, how our last fleet of hope, with our biggest ships attacked the aggressors, but it was no use. I remembered how my brother came back with the "Independence" and took me and Peter. I remember how our parents gave us their blessings. I remembered how we got married. I remembered our first night and the new life inside me. And my promise to give everything for that baby I could and everything that it needed. It felt easier. The queen let my mind go. She spoke with my in my mind again.

Do you know what you have done?

"What do you mean?

Your species has really lost its mind. You created something that has no concern for life at all. It's the only reason is to expand and grow, with no compassion, no emotion, no feelings just logic and numbers. How did you expect to control something that knows only 1 and 0?

"We made a mistake. We are sorry.

A mistake! You not only endangered yourselves, you endangered every life form.

The Queen looked at her councilors, after that one by one, they left the hall.

"Will you help us?

You were trying to play God, so you have paid for it. We are much more advanced than you in every field, but we still respect the power of the unknown. We, however, are searching for the answers for many questions about life, creation and the universe, but you are so young in your evolution and decided that you know everything, and you are "wise" enough to be masters of the universe. We will help you, but not because we want to save you. Your people made a great mess and we have to clean it up, if we don't, after a few thousand years, your uncontrollable AI will bang on our doorstep, and we will have to face a much stronger enemy than we will face now. Once, our race had three queens. We were sisters, but two of them got mad by their power and started to oppress and torture their subjects. I couldn't stand by watching these atrocities, so the big war began. There were two of them, but they were mad and their leadership abilities were weak. I won because of the loyalty of my subjects and the week and degraded armies of my enemy. After I won, my sisters were trailed and executed for their crimes; their subjects accepted my victory, and we had peace and prosperity for 3000 years. I almost forgot about those horrors, but you came along and reminded me of things that I wished to forget a long time ago. I had no other choice. The war was brought on to me, but your people brought this on yourselves. Why?

I understood that she was testing me; she was probably deciding whether to let us survive or destroy us along with the AI. So I remembered the words of professor Everton.

"We are victims of our own creations."

The queen looked at me once more and spoke again.

Hopefully next time your people will be smarter. And if not, we won't be meeting in such pleasant circumstances.

"I understand. Can I ask you a question?

Yes, you can.

"Why did the crystal only react to the light from our sun?

We are very glad to find out answers for the many questions about our universe. However, even more we respect the questions that we have no answer to. Your people are simply not ready for those answers yet. In time you will understand, but at present you just have to respect the question. Go now. My subject will lead you out.

Another Alien came along and kindly showed me the way. He showed me back to Peter and my brother. They were anxious to know what's happened.

"What is going on?" Peter asked.

"I met their Queen."

"And?" he said.

"I think they will help us."

"You think? Maybe they will kill us," said Max.

"No, they won't."

"What makes you think that?" he continued.

"I just know."

The large alien took us to an empty big field. He only took out one crystal. He put it in the air and that crystal just floated. The alien took us as far away from the crystal as he could. We could see the crystal growing. It started to form unusual shapes and different sizes. There were triangle forms, cubes, and spheres growing around that small crystal, it was growing pretty fast. I had never seen such technology. It looked like the crystal was forming into something and that something became a huge crystal ship. It was gigantic; its size was almost the size of the "Independence." The alien took us inside. It was a huge spaceship, so beautiful, different colors and distinct shapes; it was a masterpiece of light, energy, and crystals. There was an immense holo screen. We could see everything around us.

The alien did some calculations, set the course, and we jumped. We jumped right into the heat of a battle between the AI and human forces. The machines attacked the crystal ship like they attacked everything else, but the ship only absorbed the energy. They could do nothing; even the strongest of the enemy ship's lasers were absorbed. Suddenly, the alien ship fired a beam of absorbed energy back at the metallic beast ships. They went down like flies.

"I'm tired of playing these games," said the alien commander.

He entered a combination into the crystal display and after few seconds, seven small crystal probes went in all directions and jumped to the ends of our galaxy. Then some kind of the timer device kicked in. The alien looked over the display and when the seven emitter probes jumped to a right distance and when the timer stopped, he entered a code of unknown symbols into the screen and a giant EMP wave kicked in, knocking out every machine AI. Those 7 probes amplified the wave, and it hit to the remotest parts of the galaxy. I understood that even the furthest AI bases were knocked out as well.

"It's over," the commander said.

Peter and my brother hugged me. They understood that everything was over. The biggest enemy we had ever faced was defeated. In every corner of the galaxy humanity celebrated. They were happy to finally know peace. And then every human in their mind heard the most important message of their lives. It was the Queen. She used her telepathic abilities.

Humanity, you have a chance for a new beginning. Don't waste it; use it for the sake of your children. You have responsibilities now. If you think of something like this again, our encounter will not be so pleasant. I will give you a gift; very few of your people will receive it. They will feel more and know more than anyone of you. They will have the ability to read thoughts and will be the safeguards of your civilization, so value and protect them. They know more than you can imagine, you should listen to them.

"But if our leaders go mad like your sisters?" I asked,

Then you will suffer a fate that you deserve. Every action you make immediately resolves in an opposite reaction of the same magnitude. You will be judged and trailed like the machines you created. The death penalty is no exception.

"You gave us a chance. How can we repay you?"

We did it because we had to; sparing your lives was a hard decision. Don't disappoint us.

"We won't. I promise."

You just need to understand who you are and where you belong.

"What do you mean?

The future is in your hands.

"I don't understand.

In time, you will. Now just relax. My general will take you home.

The general entered the coordinates. We jumped. It was Earth; from the screens, I could see our wonderful blue planet. It was so amazing; we were back on Earth again. Thank God, everything was fine. The "Independence" jumped after a few minutes. I sent a telepathic message of gratitude to the Queen and to the General. I know they understood, but he didn't move a muscle just went aboard his ship and disappeared.

After a few years, our people sent a diplomatic mission to the same location we encountered the aliens. However, the whole planet and all the crystal technology were gone. It had disappeared, like it was never there.

That horrible war made our people rethink many things. When we understood how fragile we are, then we started to love and cherish each other more. People became closer. They understood that wars like this could never happen again. We can't let our greed and empty desires rule our minds and control our life. Darkness within our souls became a distant memory from the past and from the ashes of war, the new golden age of humanity began.

Are we still alive or are we just the shadows of our ancestors.

We have a new enemy. That menace is not looking for our money in the back alley, it's not waiting with bombs from any foreign country. It's not hidden from us in some secret organization meetings. It's the weakness in our minds and laziness in our souls. We forgot that not so long ago, our grandfathers fought in World War II for our freedoms, but now we give all our freedoms to our small screens and little boxes running on silicon chips. We forgot how to socialize, we forgot how to be human without the small pixels in a digital screen. We are slaves of our own creations. We wait for someone strong and powerful to save us, to show us the way and lead us to the wonderful future, but we are the future, we are the ones who must change, we are the only ones who are responsible for our destiny. And if we fail? We will lose everything. And only God can save us then (if we are worth saving).

Greed has conquered our minds; we became so distant from God and Mother Nature, so distant that we see only the small part of the whole, wonderful, and beautiful world surrounding us. How many of you have helped an elderly person, how many have you given to charity, or helped that blind lady cross the street. We live only for numbers in computer screens and our favorite TV shows. Some of us are so distant from reality that we spend more time online than in real life. Look outside, open the window, see how beautiful is this life. We used to play in the snow, looked amazed at the fallen leaves in autumn, listen to the birds singing, gazed at the stars, watched as swans danced in the lakes, looked at the flowers in spring and summer.

We have to fight the machine that are inside us. We have feelings. We are not automatic robots that seek only pleasure in life. If we think like cyborgs, we might end up in some virtual reality that we create for ourselves with only pleasure, fun, and fake life. After some time, we will forget what the real world looked like, until someone pulls the plug. We are bigger than that, we can feel pain sometimes and that's good, without pain once in a while, we lose the sense that we are fragile, that we are human.

The war between man and machine won't be so soon. Sooner we will face a war between the people who wish to protect life and those who see no value in it and are only blinded by greed and self-interest. We must understand that our struggle doesn't start or end in some country or some forgotten corner of the Earth. First of all, it starts in our hearts.

God made us in His image. So, are we kind and loving? Or are we addicted, stressed, overworked, with many things we don't need? Why does someone need 5 cars when he only drives one and why does someone need a house with 8 bedrooms when he sleeps in only one. If you have more than you need, share it with someone who doesn't and God will provide you with something you have never dreamed of. Jesus taught us to share with each other and love each other as brothers and sisters. If you have a Lamborghini, will you be happier when you have another one. Go to a shelter and give food to poor people. When you hand them a lump of bread, you will see their eyes filled gratitude. It will be more priceless than any new supercar in the world. Or you could visit the children's hospital and make some sick children happy, believe me you will never be happier if you do that.

However, now we think only about ourselves, so much that we don't see the truth beyond our concrete walls and between our hearts. We have the whole world within the reach of a button, but we forgot how to socialize, how to work together, how to build relationships, and how to live. Most of us spend 8 or more hours at a computer in our jobs, and then we spent the rest of our free time sitting near the same damned computer or TV screen that entertains us, gives us social life (or at least we think it does, but in reality...).

Sometimes I think we have already lost the war with the machines, but there is always hope. We forgot the value of bread on our tables, the value of the simplest cup of clean water that is given to us by our loving mother nature, and we are depleting those gifts of life continuously. Our little displays and the numbers in our bank accounts became more important to us. To many people, a piece of paper is worth more than other people, more than life. However, in the end, we might end up in a cage of our own insensibility, and then all of our hopes will be lost.

We have to remember that machines are only the reflections of our world; they represent the values that we share ourselves. If we seek war, the machines will also seek war. We must change from inside and use the technology and science to make people's lives better, not to use it for purpose of conquest or greed.

Or maybe we are at the crossroads of creating a machine that is so dangerous that we can't control it. Even now we depend on the machines too much. How many people today read books? How many people chat on the train or a bus? How many people just say hello to each other? We hope that everything will turn out fine in the end, but what if we are wrong. Maybe in the end nobody will hear us scream in the emptiness of space. Life is short, but I hope we will create a bright future for our children and not for something evil that will punish us for our stupidity. Technology has become even more important than life, faith, and God. How did we get to this point? Are we lost so much that we forgot who we are? After all, we are only human. We are fragile, and we all will face the end on this planet, but will we leave with all the riches we have found provided for us or we will leave a dead desert planet.